Fashioned for Power

Women of Power Series

Kathleen Brooks

An original work of Kathleen Brooks

Cover art by LM Creations.
http://lmbookcreations.wix.com/lm-creations

Acknowledgments

So many wonderful people gave their time to talk to me and answer questions for this book. I would like to thank Miss C for her insightful knowledge of the fashion industry. I would also like to thank Don, a great friend of mine for over twenty-five years, who answered all my questions and only laughed at a couple of them. You're a true friend. And to my dear daughter who has shown such interest and support in my writing... including helping me with names!

As always, the most important person to thank is you—the reader. Thank you for loving the Simpson family as much as I do.

Prologue

Windsor Academy High School . . .

Allegra Simpson sat quietly in the back of homeroom. Her legs were crossed under the small, attached blue tabletop. Her fingers fidgeted with the dark blue plaid skirt of her private school uniform. Raven Eddie, her archrival, was standing in front of her laughing.

"Making your own prom dress," Raven said rather than asked loud enough for the entire class to hear. "Daddy flew me to Paris to get mine, but you're making yours from a tablecloth . . . or maybe the drapes?"

"I'm not making it," Allegra said quietly. "It's my sister's, and I'm altering it."

"Why bother? No one is going to go with you. You may as well stay at home."

Allegra looked up at the queen bitch of her high school. Raven was anything but perfect. She just had big boobs and let the boys play with them. That's the only reason she was popular. That, and her daddy bribed the kids in her class with lavish parties and weekends at their mansion on a nearby lake.

"I'm going with my friend. One who likes me regardless of what I am wearing or how much my daddy pays them." Allegra felt her face flush. She wasn't used to standing up for herself. Her older sister Bree had always protected her, but Bree was now away at college along with their eldest sister, Elle. Her brother, Reid, the oldest of the four Simpson children, was off discovering himself—whatever that meant. So here she was, after seventeen years of being the baby of the family, left to fend for herself.

Raven's face turned almost purple in anger. Allegra thought it was more of a magenta color. It would make a lovely shade of ribbon for her prom dress. But then Mount Raven erupted.

"You're nothing! I dare you to come to prom. I dare you. And you can stand by looking pathetic and watch all the boys dance with me in a dress I will wear only once while you stand against the wall in a dress your sisters all wore before you. Then we'll see who has friends." Raven tossed her dirty-blond hair and stormed to the front of the room as everyone laughed.

"Mom, it was no big deal," Allegra said for the hundredth time as she bit off a length of thread with her teeth. She raised the bobbin and threaded the needle of her sewing machine. She'd discovered when she lost her temper she could be mean, and she had hated it. No matter what, Allegra Simpson would be the nice girl from now on, just like her mom had taught her.

"I'm so sorry, sweetie. You know how your father is with money. It doesn't matter that we have a little of it now; he's taken every nickel he earns and is paying for college, your schooling, and whatever we have left is going right back into the company. Just be nice. You'll win her over in the end," Margaret, Allegra's mother, said apologetically.

"Really, Mom, it's fine." Allegra pressed her foot down

on the pedal and the sewing machine came to life. She tuned out her mother and concentrated on moving the fabric slowly through the machine so her hem was straight.

"Are you listening to me?"

"No, Mom, I'm not. I'm busy."

"Honey, I have an extra two hundred dollars I've been saving . . ."

Allegra finished off the hem, and with the snip of her scissors, pulled the dress free. She flicked it with her wrists and heard her mother gasp. "See, I told you I wouldn't need a new dress."

Her mother's eyes grew large as she looked at the sea green dress. Gone were the wide straps and voluminous skirt. In its place was a soft sweetheart neckline to accentuate Allegra's breasts. They weren't as large as Raven's, but they were supple and perky. The sides had been taken in to accent Allegra's small waist, and those lines continued down the length of the dress to where the skirt tapered into a slender fit along her hips and long legs. Allegra had cut a long slit up one leg to show it off when she walked.

"That color is going to be breathtaking with your hair," Margaret whispered as she eyed the dress.

Allegra had counted on it. While Elle had red hair like her mother, Allegra had blonde hair like Bree. So she'd asked Bree if she could have her old prom dress. The blue tint to the green caused her clear blue eyes to sparkle.

Allegra slid into the dress and turned her back for her mother to zip it up. It fit like a glove. Allegra smiled into the mirror. Clothes had a way of making her feel good about herself. It didn't matter how much they cost or where they came from. It mattered how they fit, their color, and their personality. It was like they talked to her. She could be herself with them. And this dress was the real Allegra. Now she just had to have the courage to wear it out of the house.

The hotel ballroom was packed with sparkly dresses and boys in black tuxedos. It was a thrill for Allegra's senses. She smiled as she saw dresses she'd love to make dance by her.

"Here goes nothing," Nate Reece said as he held out his arm. Allegra smiled at her best friend and placed her arm on his. Nate and Allegra had been best friends since freshman year drama class. In a month he was heading to New York City, and she was going to design school in California.

Allegra and Nate made their way to the dance floor as people cast them surprised looks. Allegra had taken the liberty of adjusting Nate's rental tux so it showed how good-looking he really was. Nate liked to hide behind baggy pants and layers of shirts. While he didn't have the body of an athlete, it did hold promise, just like Nate himself did.

"I can't wait to be out of this school," Nate muttered as some of the dancers around them started whispering. "At least it got me into that acting school."

"Soon we can leave this all behind. I can get lost in the masses at college and you will be on stage performing in front of thousands of people. Promise you won't forget me," Allegra teased.

"I could never forget you. If it hadn't been for you and your friendship, I would never have made it through all the snobbery. Speaking of which, here comes the queen bee."

"I'm going to have to apologize. I was so mean to her

this morning," Allegra started to say before stopping to stare at a dress only an angel could have made.

"Raven," Allegra whispered in a gasp. "That dress is amazing. Look at the way it's made. And the layering. The texture!"

Allegra was so wrapped up in her lovefest with Raven's dress she didn't see the victorious look on Raven's face.

With a smile of pure satisfaction, Raven did a quick spin in her dress. "Well, now that you know you can't compete, I'm going to dance."

"That dress is a work of art," Allegra said wistfully as Raven sashayed toward her date.

"I can't believe you." Nate shook his dark brown hair as he slid his hand over her back and brought her back into the dance.

"What?"

"You're too nice."

"Is there such a thing as too nice?"

"Yes. Your sisters taught me that. But I think you were too busy playing dress-up to hear their lessons. Raven will never respect you. She won. You practically orgasmed when you saw her dress."

"It was a great dress, and it's not like I'm getting any from anyone else. That dress is the thrill of my night," Allegra joked.

Nate just shook his head. "Someday being nice won't be enough. Mark my words. Someday you'll get in trouble for being such a pushover."

Chapter One

Twelve years later . . .

Allegra closed her eyes and savored the moment. The sounds of the band surrounded her along with the voices of happy conversation and laughter. Warm strong arms encircled her as she swayed side to side. She felt his muscular legs rub against her to the rhythm of the slow song. His hand tightened on her hip and pulled her closer to him. Heaven was being in Finn Williams's embrace.

"Hey, Leggy. We're out of here." Her sister Bree laughed, calling Allegra by her childhood nickname.

Reluctantly Allegra lifted her head from Finn's broad shoulder to smile at her sister. The wedding dress Allegra had made for Bree was nothing compared to the smile on her face. Allegra had gained another brother-in-law that evening. Elle, her oldest sister and CEO of Simpson Global, had married sexy tech genius Drake Charles last year. Now her other sister, Bree, had married the devastatingly handsome architect Logan Ward.

Allegra stepped away from Finn's warmth to hug her sister and then Logan. They were so perfect together. Bree had always been the tough-as-nails sibling with a wild streak. That's what it took to run a billion-dollar steel and construction company. But it seemed Logan's steady nature had centered her. They were happy and clearly in love.

"Congratulations," Allegra whispered to Bree as she hugged her tightly. She was feeling somewhat alone tonight—she and Reid were the only unmarried Simpsons.

Allegra was nothing like Bree. She lived in a world of beauty, not dirt. After their father died, the reins to the burgeoning company had been turned over to Elle, who had to fight off takeovers to grow the company into the multibillion-dollar global conglomerate it was today. After Allegra had finished college and design school, she had joined her brother at the company run by their two older sisters. They had given her the freedom to grow her love of fashion and design. Now Allegra ran one of the largest parent companies in the fashion world, on top of having her own small fashion house.

"Thank you, Leggy. For this dress and everything you did to set this wedding up—it is a dream come true," Bree said with a tear in her eye that she quickly wiped away.

"David and Josh are so into dancing over there, I didn't get a chance to thank them for making the tux for me. Please thank them for me," Logan told her as he kissed her cheek and shook Finn's hand.

Bree looked between them and then smiled. "Well, we're jumping ship. Enjoy the privacy of the island. And Finn . . ."

"Yes?"

"Take care of my sister, will ya?"

Finn's deep brown eyes glowed with delight. He was just as quick as she at picking up her sister's approval of them together. Allegra felt her heart plummet at the feel of her phone vibrating in her purse. The slow steady vibration brought her back to reality. She could never be with Finn. It didn't matter that she was head over heels in love with him; she couldn't share her heart right now.

"With pleasure." Finn looked into her face and smiled.

Bree smiled again, and with a wave the newlyweds disappeared to the other end of the private island the Simpson family owned off the Connecticut coast.

"Oh, it was such a beautiful night," her mother said as she clapped her hands. Margaret Simpson was the epitome of Southern class. She'd had it when they were dirt-poor, and she had it now that they were one of the richest families in the world. Margaret believed money was inconsequential to good manners.

"It was, without a doubt, Mrs. Simpson," Finn said.

"Knock off that *Mrs.* stuff, Finn. We're practically family." With a wink to Finn, she hurried over to talk to Reid.

Finn slid his arm around Allegra's waist and pulled her toward him again, but he'd lost her in that one split second. For a minute, he thought he had a chance with a girl like her. When she melted against his body and he had wrapped his arms around her, he thought she was showing him some interest. But now she was as stiff as a board in his arms.

With a sigh, Finn pulled away and looked at his dream woman. She was distracted and looking anywhere but at his face. "How about I get you a drink?"

Allegra jerked her head up and nodded absently before turning to pull her phone from her small purse.

Finn gave her one last wistful look before making his way through the crowd as he headed toward the bar. The night was clear and stars twinkled above the dance floor on the estate's lawn. The clearing was surrounded by woods on one side and the ocean on the other. Strategically placed gas lanterns provided a warm glow, chasing the chill from the fall air. The walk to the bar gave him time to think about Allegra. His heart was already invested. He had fallen in love with her months ago and had done everything he could to be near her. Her positivity and sweetness were contagious. He found himself craving her smiles and the gentle ringing of her laughter. His six-foot-two-inch body could be brought to its knees by one of her smiles. But, he was receiving mixed messages.

Finn had made it a long way in his thirty-four years, but not far enough to be a part of this crowd. He knew the Simpsons had been poor once. But he doubted they had to fight the constant battle of drugs, alcohol, and the low expectations he had to confront growing up. But he had done it. His mother had scraped by on two jobs and made sure he went to school every day and that he was at the ball field for baseball practice every night.

It had paid off when he got a baseball scholarship to college. After two years, he was drafted and sent to a minor league team to scrape his way up to the big leagues. He was almost there. He was set to be called up. He knew it, and to show off he made a stupid decision. He tore every ligament in his knee as he tried to make an acrobatic catch on a routine pop-up. He lost everything in one second. Looking across the small dance floor, he saw Allegra's back to him and knew in this one second he had just lost something more special to him than baseball had ever been.

Allegra's hand shook as message after message came pouring onto the screen of her phone.

Whore. Whore. Whore.

Tears spilled down her cheeks as she fumbled with the

phone to turn it off. *Whore. Whore. Whore.*

"Allegra, are you all right?"

Allegra shoved the phone back into her purse and wiped her tears away before turning around to give a shaky smile to Elle and Drake. "Fine, why?" Oh God, don't let them talk to me for long, Allegra wished.

"You look like you've seen a ghost," Drake said as he looked around for Elle's former driver. "Did Finn do something to upset you?"

After being hurt in baseball, Finn had started driving a taxi. The night their father died, he'd picked up Elle and driven her to the hospital. He'd stayed outside waiting for her and driven Allegra's distraught sister home afterward. Soon Elle had hired him to be her driver at Simpson Global, as well as paying for him to finish his degree at night school. After earning a bachelor's degree, Finn went on to more night classes at law school. Once he'd passed the Bar, he approached Elle with the idea for Simpson Global to buy a failing sports management agency and turn it into an all-around entertainment agency. Elle looked over the proposal Allegra had helped Finn prepare and agreed. Finn was a ballplayer who turned into VP of Simpson Entertainment, and Allegra was in love with him.

"No!" Allegra said quickly, startling them both. Elle didn't blink, but Drake raised a dark eyebrow at her. "Um, he's just getting me a drink. I was lost in thought about Fashion Week. You know how crazy this time of year is for me."

"Drake, can you get me a drink, too?" Elle asked sweetly. Oh, no. Allegra was about to get a lecture.

"Um, sure?" Drake answered and when his wife nodded he sauntered off to meet Finn at the bar.

"Okay, spill it."

"Spill what?" Allegra asked innocently.

Elle rolled her green eyes at her. "You were the same way when Raven picked on you during high school, and you refused to tell us because you knew we'd chew you out for being too nice."

"Sometimes it pays to be nice," Allegra argued back.

"Sometimes, but not all the time. Who have you been too nice to now?"

"I don't know what you mean," Allegra said, knowing full well what she meant.

"One," Elle put up her finger, "Stephanie Manicheck, your college roommate who walked all over you and stole money from you. Yet, you refused to kick her out because you're a pushover. Two," Elle held up another finger, "Lewis Blackwater."

"He was brokenhearted," Allegra mumbled.

"You broke up with him by giving him flowers and telling him how wonderful his cheating ass was. Then he guilt-tripped you into paying for a trip to Vegas in order for him to get over you. While there, he knocked up a showgirl and asked you to make her wedding dress . . . which you did!"

"Fine," Allegra said sharply. "I'm too nice. Is that what you want to hear?"

"No. I want you to stand up for yourself. And if you can't, then at least have the courage to tell me or Bree so we can help."

"So you can run my life, you mean. Take care of poor little Leggy."

Elle crossed her arms over the chest Allegra wished she had and narrowed her eyes. "You know damn well that's not what I am talking about. I'm worried about you. You've been acting strangely since you broke up with that loser,

Harry, last year. You isolated yourself. I thought you were getting better and dating Finn, but you aren't. Are you?"

Allegra looked away. Sometimes having sisters was hard. She wished they could all be as blissfully ignorant as Reid. Brothers . . . they never noticed anything. "No, I'm not dating Finn. Why is everyone pushing me to date him? Did it ever occur to any of you that I don't want to date him?"

"Here's your drink. I'm heading back home tonight. Sorry to have bothered you." Allegra whirled around to see Finn and Drake standing behind her. Finn's dark skin glowed a soft brown in the romantic lights, and his eyes were masked in shadows. He shoved the glass at her. The cold liquid splashed on her hand as he turned sharply on his heel and strode away from her.

"I always thought you were the nice one," Drake said, his voice full of censure.

Allegra slammed the glass on the table. She noticed Reid and her mother look over with surprise. "What you don't know is that I am being nice. I'm protecting Finn from nothing but trouble. Now, excuse me. I need to work on the after-party at Fashion Week."

Allegra stormed into the woods. She felt the branches tear at the soft wispy dress she'd made, but she didn't care. She kept going until she pushed through to the other side of the small island. Waves from the Long Island Sound slapped against the large rocks lining the island. She kicked off her heels and took a tentative step onto the closest rock. It was cold. It matched her heart. She carefully made it farther out so she could look directly down into the water. Wind whipped her hair as she took a seat on the massive rock. Waves splashed against the boulders and drops of water cascaded down onto her.

She looked out in the distance and refused to even

blink. There. Two red taillights just appeared on the mainland. Finn. She watched him turn his car on and drive away. She didn't move until they had turned so small she could no longer see them. Her hopes and dreams of a future—of love—just disappeared with Finn.

This was her life now—one of loneliness and sleepless nights. She'd done it to herself when she'd broken up with Harry. He'd tried to get back with her in person and when she rejected him, he started asking her out through anonymous texts and emails. When she rejected him again, politely, things changed. She felt him watching her on the streets; she felt him staring at her at the gym. But whenever she looked around, she never saw him. And the texts changed. He told her he knew she loved him and knew she wanted to be with him, but was a whore for seeing other people—Finn, her personal trainer, and the man at the coffee shop. Somehow she had to fix this herself. Allegra opened her purse and turned on her phone. Hundreds of text messages started pinging. *Whore. Whore. Whore. Whore. Whore.*

Finn drove along the coast with the windows down. His hands gripped the wheel tightly as he let the cold fury overtake him. Getting angry was better than feeling the pain of his heart breaking. He shouldn't be surprised though. He had known he wasn't good enough for her. But he had prayed that Allegra was different. He had thought she didn't care where he came from or how much money he had—or didn't have. But he was wrong.

He didn't know how long it took, but soon he was at the small private airfield. The Simpson jet stood by to carry partygoers home in the morning. Allegra would be with them, and he didn't think he could see her right then.

"Finn? What are you doing here so late?"

Finn sighed with relief at the voice of the Simpson's tough pilot. "Troy. Just the man I was looking for. An emergency has come up, and I need to get back to Atlanta."

"Sure. Let me file the flight plan, and we can be on our way shortly. I'll be back in plenty of time to pick the others up tomorrow."

Finn followed Troy up the stairs of the private jet and sat down in the soft leather chair. Through the pain of the night, something else was bothering him. If he thought it through, then it might come to him. But as he opened the bar and poured a whiskey, he decided thinking was overrated.

Chapter Two

Finn got out of the cab and stared down the street he'd grown up on. He swayed as he took a step toward his mother's split-level house. Bright yellow mums were planted by the sidewalk. The nicely kept home was in stark contrast to the run-down rental house next door. Finn's neighborhood was a mix of low-income families. Some tried to make the best of life. They worked hard, sent their kids to school, went to church every week, and watched out for their neighbors. Others loved their community as well, just in a different way. It was naïve to think all their activities were legal. But they always seemed to support the community and the youngsters who showed promise. They just didn't care about mowing their yard every week or fixing broken shutters.

Finn saw the group of guys he'd grown up with sitting on their porch drinking beer and laughing. At thirteen, he'd wanted to be them. He'd snuck out of the house one night, sauntered down the street as if he were tough, and sat down with them.

"What the hell are you doing?" Terrell had asked.

"I'm having a beer," Finn had said nonchalantly as he'd picked one up out of a cooler.

"Don't you have school tomorrow?"

Finn had just shrugged. Terrell and the guys had

shaken their heads at him.

"Put that down and get back to bed. Your ma will tan your hide if she catches you out here. And I might too if you don't get your ass back to your house."

Finn had felt crushed. He had been excluded again. The only place he'd felt like himself was the ball field. Now he couldn't even fit in on his own street. "But, you all don't go to school."

"Exactly and look at us. But you, Finn Williams, have a gift. You are meant for more than sitting around drinking beer. If you want to come by after school and shoot some hoops, we'll be around." Finn had quickly nodded his head and had left. At least he had still been part of the group.

From that point on, after school he would come home, do his homework, go down to Mrs. Jones's house for some cookies, and then go to play ball with Terrell and the guys until his mom picked him up for baseball practice. It seemed Terrell and his mother had some kind of unspoken agreement. Terrell helped Finn keep his nose clean and Finn's mom made sure Terrell and the guys always had a home-cooked meal on her day off from work.

But as Finn made his way past his mother's house and toward Terrell, the last thing he was thinking about was being the good guy his mother had raised him to be. No, good guys finished last. Good guys got their hearts broken. He was done being the good guy.

"Finn? What the hell are you doing here?" Terrell asked as he stood up and came down the steps of his porch. "Are you drunk?"

Finn stopped walking and swayed. "Sure am. And I'm only getting started." He looked around the street he'd grown up on. It seemed quiet tonight. There should be a party around here somewhere. "Where are those girls? The ones that always strut around here?"

Terrell grabbed his arm to steady him. "Finn, what's going on?"

"It's all good. I'm just looking for a drink and some friendly company."

"What happened? You never act like this. You have too much to lose to start down this path now."

Finn leaned forward and put a finger to his lips. "I'll tell you a secret. I've already lost it all." He paused and cocked his head. "Can you lose something you never had in the first place?"

"Why can't you have it?"

"I didn't go to private school. My family isn't old money. I'm too nice. That's it, Terrell; I'm too nice."

Terrell shook his head. "Man, you ain't too nice. I've seen you in a fistfight. So, you went and fell in love with a little rich girl?"

Finn frowned and nodded his head.

"And she doesn't want you? You're a good catch. Does she know you run that fancy company?"

Finn grimaced. "She owns part of that fancy company."

"You fell in love with your boss?"

"Well, not really my boss, but a Simpson. She's way too good for me, man. I knew she was out of my league. But there were signs, ya know?"

"Come on, Finn. Have a beer and tell us all about her." Terrell slapped his shoulder and led him up the porch.

Allegra's whole body was shaking. The sun was rising over the ocean. She hadn't moved from the rock all night. She was damp, cold, and scared. The texts had come all night long—thousands of them. She had taken a screen shot of them, emailed it to herself, and then had thrown the phone into the ocean.

She needed to go to the police. She needed to get a restraining order. She needed to get Finn back. But instead, Allegra just sat there. It was overwhelming. She felt as if she were one of those rocks constantly being smashed by wave after wave. She struggled to breathe as her chest tightened. The panic attack she'd kept at bay all night was hitting her now as the light of a new day dawned.

Her breath came in short pants as she lay down in a small ball on the rock. "Breathe, it'll pass," Allegra repeated in her mind over and over again. Her mother had taught her to be nice, and nice girls don't need restraining orders. Allegra Simpson, head of a major fashion empire, couldn't be so weak as to need help against a single man. What would her investors think? What would her designers think? But the overwhelming factor that stopped her from getting up was knowing her sisters would look at her with sympathy.

No, she had to handle it herself. She'd caused the problem. She would have to fix it alone.

Allegra wiped her nose with the tissue and sniffled. She tried to hide her nerves as she took a shaky sip of her hot tea and waited. It had been three days since she spent the night on the rock watching Finn drive out of her life. When the sun came up that morning, she knew she had to make the first move. Allegra had sent an email and set up a time to set things straight. She almost screamed when a hand grabbed her shoulder from behind.

She whipped around and looked into the slightly droopy eyes of her ex-boyfriend, Harry Daniels. They had met online. His profile picture was of a six-foot man with chiseled features and a bright smile. When they met up, she found a man of average height with below-average looks. He was an accountant. But he had a sense of humor, so she allowed the date to continue despite the deception.

"Allegra. Golly, it's good to see you again. I knew you would come back to me." Allegra shivered. Of course he knew. He'd been sending her texts from an unlisted number since they broke up. He'd been terrorizing her daily.

"Are you all right? You look sick. Let me take care of you. You never could take care of yourself," Harry clucked.

Allegra felt the familiar defeat. He'd always pointed out what she couldn't do. He used it to beat her down and make her think she couldn't do anything without him. He'd exploded when she'd finally had enough strength to break up with him.

"It's just a cold, Harry. Please sit down. We need to talk."

"Of course, dumplin'." Harry shook his head as he looked her over. "You sure haven't been keeping yourself up. Look at you, all pale and puffy."

Allegra ground her teeth together and looked at the man she had thought was harmless. "Harry, you need to leave me alone, or I'll call the police."

Harry's eyes showed concern as his brow knitted together. "Leave you alone? I haven't seen you since we broke up. You're the one who called me here today."

"I'm talking about the emails and the text messages. You're harassing me and it has to stop—now," Allegra said as forcefully as she could.

"Dumplin', those were forever ago. And then I was only trying to find out why you broke up with me. I thought you called me here today to get back together."

"That will *never* happen. Do you understand?" Allegra growled.

"Then why did you call me here?"

"To tell you to leave me alone. I don't buy for one second that it's not you sending me those messages to threaten Finn and me."

"Finn?" Harry asked with an edge to his voice. "So, you're already dating someone new?"

"As if you don't know that. We broke up almost a year ago. You know I've dated a couple of guys since then. You've spent that time trying to win me back, and then you started threatening me . . . harassing me. Move on, Harry. I have. Now, I'm going to say this once. Leave me the hell alone." Allegra stood so forcefully her chair tipped over. Everyone in the coffee shop turned and stared as she stormed away.

She had done it. She had stood up for herself. Allegra let out a deep breath as she made her way to get a new phone with a new number. Right now, a moving company was loading boxes into a van and moving her across town. She'd found a house in the warehouse district close to Bree and a couple of the small clothing boutiques she owned. No one knew her new number or address, and it was going to stay that way. Taking a deep breath, Allegra felt free for the first time in a year.

Finn's office door slammed, causing him to grab his head and groan. He'd gone on a two-day bender trying to numb the pain in his heart. It hadn't helped. In fact, it had just made it worse.

He cracked an eye and saw a shiny walker with *Original*

Sex Goddess hanging on it. Original was right. The owner of the walker probably knew Aphrodite.

Shirley, the ancient office manager for Simpson Global, stopped her walker in front of Finn's desk and took a seat. "What are you doing?"

"Go away, Shirley," Finn muttered as he closed his eyes. The next second, a loud honking noise shot him up from his chair in surprise. Shirley smiled devilishly and threatened to honk the huge horn she had on her walker again.

"Stop! How can you stand that awful noise?"

Shirley looked at him strangely, put her finger in her ear, and turned on her hearing aid. "I'm sorry, dear. What did you say?"

Finn let out a long-suffering breath and flopped back into his chair.

"Are you trying to mess up the best thing you could ever have?"

"Not you too," Finn groaned. "First Terrell and now you. Where's Mrs. Simpson? I'm sure she'll be in here soon to tell me what I failure I am."

"Would you like some cheese with that whine?"

Finn glared at the old woman sitting happily across from him, but it didn't scare her. Actually, he had a feeling Shirley would tell the devil himself to mind his manners.

"If you're done pouting, we need to talk."

"About what? Allegra made it perfectly clear she didn't want to be with me."

Shirley slid her dentures around absently and then slammed her mouth shut in a thin line. "I heard all about it from Elle. Something is not right. Allegra told Elle she was protecting you. I've seen the two of you together, and there's something there. Trust me."

Shirley's words slowly penetrated the fog in his mind. "Wait, she said she was protecting me?"

"Yes. Something is going on. Something she's not telling anyone. But the only reason she'd say something harsh like that just to protect you means she cares about you."

Finn thought about it for a minute. That was what had been bothering him ever since that night. Her reaction was so un-Allegra . . . so desperate. "I think you're right. Excuse me, Shirley, I have to see someone right away."

He dialed the phone and smiled. He had her just where he wanted her. His wife would be in his arms and under him in his bed whether she liked it or not. Even if she had spread her legs for that scum, Finn, he'd purify his Allegra and teach her the proper way for his wife to act. She was destined to be his and his alone. The feeling was so strong, and he knew she felt it, too. She was just scared of those feelings. She was a part of his heart and soon would be more than that.

"I'm sorry, the number you are trying to reach is not in service," a woman's automated voice said over the phone.

"That bitch!" He slammed the prepaid phone down on his desk. If she thought she could shut him out of her life just like that, she had another think coming. She was *his*. He grew excited as he thought about how he was going to punish her. Oh yes, he was going to enjoy teaching her a lesson. He was going to woo his wife into his life and his bed before showing her who was really in control.

Chapter Three

Allegra smiled to her driver as she stepped out of her car and onto the sidewalk in front of Simpson Global. Her line was complete for Fashion Week. She'd just met with the last of her designers and the casting directors who were heading off to New York soon to start interviewing the models. Things were falling in place. And since she moved and changed her phone number, she hadn't received a single threatening text. Finally, she slept all night long.

"Allegra?"

Allegra looked to the deep voice calling her name and smiled. "Asher! What a pleasant surprise. I haven't seen you since Blythe's Valentine's dinner party. How are you?"

The handsome man in a tailor-made suit stopped and smiled down at her. He was sinfully attractive with his black hair and emerald green eyes. He was old Atlanta money, the Southern version of the Rockefellers. His job was to be the heir of the empire. Empire of what, Allegra wasn't sure. It was why she and Asher had never dated. He'd asked, but she'd declined politely. They just cared about different things. He cared about having his face all over the society pages, traveling the world, and wasting his huge trust fund. But, they'd managed to strike a friendship. Probably because he was so easygoing it was hard not to like him.

"I'm good. Just been traveling. I was in Monaco the other week with the Princess of Denmark. I'm surprised I didn't see Reid there."

"He's busy starting a resort here in Atlanta. It's almost done from what he's said. You'll have to come to the grand opening."

"As your date?" Asher grinned.

Allegra rolled her eyes playfully. "Ha! I saw the picture of you in *Page Six*. I'd need to grow another five inches, lose twenty pounds, and perfect the indifferent stare to be one of your dates."

Asher laughed, and Allegra felt good. The past year had been hard on her, and now she finally felt as if she could put them behind her.

"You know, Jasper has been asking about you. I think you've made an impression on him."

"Jasper?" Allegra felt her eyes widen. There was nothing wrong with Jasper. He was just anti-social. She couldn't imagine sitting through a date with him. "He barely said three words to me at Blythe's."

"Then those three words must have left quite the impression." Asher licked his bottom lip and smirked. Allegra rolled her eyes and playfully smacked his arm.

"I'm sorry to interrupt, but I need a moment, Allegra."

Allegra stiffened at the voice behind her and the hand that cupped her elbow. Finn. She flushed with shame at the way she'd treated him. She just didn't know how she was going to say she was sorry. What she had done was unforgivable.

"You are interrupting," Asher said coldly in her defense.

Allegra put her hand on Asher's arm. "It's okay, Asher.

I need to talk to him as well. It was so good seeing you. Will I see you at Fashion Week?"

"Models, parties, you . . . nothing would keep me away." He winked.

"Good. I'll send you an invitation to my party. See you then." Allegra watched Asher shoot Finn a warning glare and then walk off down the sidewalk.

"Who was that prick?" Finn asked with barely controlled anger.

"That's none of your business," Allegra shot back. Finn felt her anger and knew he'd messed up. He had come to convince her to trust him enough to tell him what was going on, then he came in here and ruined it. But, when he saw that man looking at her like that . . .

"He wants to sleep with you."

"Of course he does. Asher wants to sleep with everyone. Well, maybe not you."

"And yet you invite him to your fashion party? I don't like him."

"I don't care what you like, Finn. Actually, he was telling me about someone else interested in me. The more important question is why are you being like this?" Allegra asked.

It was a good question. He'd spent the whole weekend trying to forget her—trying to get her out of his mind. But she wasn't going anywhere. He knew the second he looked at her he should run and protect his heart. But when her eyes met his, he knew there was no way he could walk away.

"Because I care about you, Allegra. I'm sorry, but I want what is best for you. And he's not it."

"And what's best for me?" Allegra asked. He thought

he heard the hope in the question. Could she care?

"Leggy!"

Dear God, not another guy. Finn saw a tall man with gelled brown hair rush up to Allegra and wrap her in a huge hug. Allegra's face lit with joy as she clung to him. Finn felt his heart drop. This man was different from Asher. This was a man she cared about. This was why she was trying to warn him off. She was taken.

"We'll talk later, Allegra. Just remember, I'll always be a friend to you if you need me," Finn said quietly once the man finally put Allegra down.

"Wait—" Allegra started to say, but Finn couldn't take the pain of seeing her in this man's arms.

"I have a meeting with Kane Royale. I have some deals lined up for him. I'll talk to you later." Finn left the happy couple embracing on the sidewalk and headed for his office. He would have to work to wipe her from his memory, but he didn't think he would be able to. Her name was already engraved on his soul. She was happy, and that was the most important thing. He just wished she were happy with him.

Allegra watched Finn walk into Simpson Global. His back was stiff, and she felt the pain from the argument. She desperately wanted to run to him—tell him she loved him. But her emotions were all over the place. She felt free from her tormentor, but was she really? And what was with Finn's attitude?

"Did I interrupt something there?"

"Oh, Nate! I'm so glad you're here. I have so much to tell you."

Her best friend smiled at her and gave her a wink. "I do, too. Guess who landed the lead in the next summer blockbuster action movie?"

"The one I helped you learn lines for?"

"The very one. I got the part."

Allegra jumped into Nate's arms and gave him a squeeze. "Congratulations!"

"And you will never believe whose daddy called me to see if I needed a date to the red carpet."

"Whose?'

"Raven Eddie's."

Allegra's eyes grew round, and then she doubled over laughing. "No way!"

"Yes, way. Can you believe it?"

"Did you tell him you're gay?"

"Hell no. That is a closely guarded secret."

"I still don't understand why."

"Come on, we have a lot to talk about. First, I want to hear all about that hunk who stormed off, and then I'll tell you all about having to hide that I'm gay in order to be an action star."

"Dumbass." Finn banged his head on his desk.

"I'd say you are if you keep doing that." Kane Royale laughed from the doorway.

"Shut up. You found love with your model."

"And I thought you found love with my lady's boss. But I guess not, hence the head banging."

Finn just groaned. He'd known Kane for years. It didn't matter that he was the star wide receiver for the Atlanta Golden Eagles. He was the most down-to-earth guy Finn had ever known. He came from a similar background as Finn. They'd been friends ever since they met at Tigo's gym. In fact, it was Kane who had planted the seed in Finn's mind to start his own sports agency. Finn took the idea and ran with it. He turned the sports agency into an entertainment agency and now represented actors, athletes, recording artists, and models.

"She runs hot and cold. Right now it's so cold I've been frozen out."

"Want to have our business meeting at Tigo's?"

Finn looked up at Kane and smiled. Going to the gym and talking business during a round of boxing sounded perfect to him. One way or another, he would forget about Allegra Simpson.

"So, you love him," Nate said as he sipped the champagne Allegra had uncorked.

"I do, but with those threats . . ."

"You need to tell him. And you need to report those. I had a stalker once and it was scary. She broke into my house. Thank goodness I was away on location."

"This isn't a stalker. Just an unhappy man."

Nate raised his perfectly sculpted eyebrow. "Honey, this is a stalker, and he's dangerous. Promise me you'll call the police, or I'll tell your sisters."

Allegra almost dropped her glass. "You wouldn't?"

"In this case I would. You're my best friend, and I can't sit by and do nothing. Either you call the police or I'll call Elle."

"But then they'll all know I can't take care of myself. They'll all tell me how I should have listened to them."

"So what? What's a little sisterly nose-rubbing when your life is at risk?"

"Fine. I'll call the police," Allegra said through gritted teeth.

"Now." Nate held out his cell phone, and Allegra called the one person she knew would help her without saying anything.

"Hello, Damien. I was hoping you wouldn't mind stopping by my house when you get off." Allegra gave Agent Damien Wallace of the Secret Service her new address. He'd helped her family a couple of times before, and she felt comfortable enough with him to ask his advice. After saying goodbye, Allegra turned back to Nate.

"Now, tell me why you want me to get you a date with one of the models," Allegra said after hanging up the phone.

Nate rolled his eyes. "My agent says if I want action hero roles I have to be straight. Sex still sells. You should know that. And the man they want saving the world can't be gay. So, please, don't out me."

"I would never out you. But that's not fair to ask you to change who you are."

"Please, as if it would change who I was. I'll just be quiet about it."

"Well, I know a model from a tiny Eastern European country who doesn't even speak English. You all can just smile at each other for the cameras, and it will be perfect. I'll arrange pictures with lots of models at my after-party. It shouldn't be a problem when you're the hottest star in Hollywood."

"Thank you. Now, I think you should call Finn."

Allegra took another sip of her drink. "I don't think I'm ready. Is that strange? I love him, yet I know I'm not ready to love him. I feel as if I'm not me yet."

"I went through that when I was trying to come to grips with my sexuality. Are you sure you're not a lesbian?" Nate teased.

"I'm sure." Allegra laughed. "Here I've done so much on my own, but I'm scared. I never let myself think of a future with Finn. I fell in love and closed my heart to him to protect him. Until I feel comfortable that this whole thing with Harry is over, I'm scared to even think about a happily-ever-after. That is, if he'll even talk to me after the way I've treated him."

Finn threw a jab followed by a left hook on Kane's jaw. Sweat dripped down his bare chest and the ridges of his abdomen as he and Kane circled each other in Tigo's boxing ring.

"Ouch."

"Sorry, I didn't mean to hit you that hard," Finn told Kane.

"No, not the punch . . . the part about Allegra in another guy's arms. I only met her a couple times here at the gym, but I didn't take her for that kind of girl."

"The kind who makes a guy think he's the only man for her and then leaps into the arms of someone else?"

"Yeah, exactly. Hey, we have that commercial to film during Fashion Week, right?"

"For the sports drink," Finn told him as he ducked a punch.

"So, you'll be in New York with me. Why don't you hit some of the parties with me? I'm sure my girl has some single friends."

Finn thought of Allegra's smile as that man twirled her around. He didn't even feel the punch Kane landed. Maybe that was the way to get her out of his mind—find someone new. "Sure. Let's do it. I can stand a couple more weeks here. It's not like Allegra and I run in the same circles."

"Are you sure about that? I mean, you brought her here, and now she comes every morning."

"Dammit. It looks like I'll be moving my workouts to

the evening."

"You're such a wimp. Scared of a little slip of a girl."

"You would be, too, if you loved her as much as I do. She has the power to hurt me more than anyone else ever could."

Allegra printed off the screen shot of the texts Harry had sent her and handed them to Damien.

"Where's the phone?"

"In the Long Island Sound."

"It would have helped to have it."

"I can see if the gardener can find it. I know where I threw it, but with the waves . . ."

"No, I just want you to sign this so I can get the records from your phone company." Damien Wallace shoved a form in front of her to sign. He'd been ticked off since he arrived, and his stiff posture showed her he was still angry.

"Are you mad at me?" Allegra asked as she signed the form.

"Hell yeah, I am. I know Mallory and I broke up, but I thought we were friends. You should have told me about this when you got the first text message. Did you at least tell Mallory?" Damien asked, referring to Elle's best friend who ran security for Simpson Global.

Allegra shook her head. This was why she didn't tell them. She would always be the baby of the family they felt needed to be looked after.

"This guy sounds dangerous. I want a list of who it could be. I'll look into it myself and pass the information to the state police."

"What if it's a burner phone?"

"Then it will take longer to get the evidence we need. If he contacts you again, try not to throw the evidence into the drink," Damien said as he stood up. "Look, Allegra, I'm sorry to get mad. But women seem to think it's their fault men stalk them so they end up not reporting it. These guys can be dangerous. Sure, sometimes all they want is to grab your panties and sell them online. But most of the time they can be deadly. Especially if they think they have a claim on you. You never know what will set them off. I want you to get some protection—pepper spray or something. Promise."

Allegra nodded. She'd see Tigo in the morning and ask about self-defense lessons. "I promise, so long as you promise not to tell Mallory or my family. I need to handle this myself."

"Fine. I'll call you as soon as I have anything. Stay aware and follow your gut. If something seems wrong, call me."

Allegra led Damien out the door and made sure to lock it. It was silly to be so scared, but maybe Damien was right. Maybe she did need to protect herself. With determination, Allegra set out her gym clothes for the morning and decided to make a stop to pick up some pepper spray on the way to work tomorrow.

Chapter Four

Allegra closed the last suitcase and stood up to survey her closet. Fashion Week was a nightmare. While she enjoyed the fashion, the industry, and the beauty of it all, not everyone else did. Most thought of it as a competition. They bustled around New York City in outrageous clothes, trying to one-up each other. Allegra had gotten the shock of her life the first time she went.

Always the nice girl, it was a huge surprise to her that fashion heads and designers were nothing but fierce competitors with each other. No one cared if she said hello. They were too interested in creating buzz, being with their cliques, and ignoring the new girl in town. And as much as Allegra fought against it, when she went to New York, she now focused on her people, her cliques, and the massive party she threw for her houses.

But this year was going to be different. During the past couple of weeks, she had gained a new outlook on life. She'd been able to sleep better, to think, and to grow as a person. Her talk with Harry had worked. He hadn't sent any more text messages or emails. She loved her new house and spent nights alone decorating it. In the mornings, she met Tigo for self-defense lessons. She felt her confidence grow with each class. She could stand on her own two feet. She could yell, kick, and punch. Tigo had immediately found her weaknesses and pushed her until she screamed at the top of her lungs for the first time in her life. And now she could say no. She could be strong. She was woman, and everyone would hear her roar.

The knock on her door surprised her. For a moment, she worried Harry had found her. But, no, he was too much of a coward to taunt her face to face. Damien had called every week. The phone that had contacted her was a burner phone from Atlanta. They were trying to track down video footage, but the store didn't have cameras. The man paid with cash, so no tracking by credit card. Allegra figured Harry had been careful. Since her chat with him, she'd been left alone.

Allegra hauled her suitcase off the bed and wheeled it to join the six others by the front door. Allegra opened the door and smiled at Shirley. "Hey! Are you here to wish me luck?"

Shirley wheeled into the house with her walker and banner reading *PSA – Package Security Agent* on it. "No, I'm here to knock some sense into you." Shirley hefted her massive purse and swung it against her arm. Allegra fell backward from the hit.

"Jeez, what do you have in there?"

"Oh, a little of this and that. Now, what the heck are you doing screwing up your life?"

"What? I've been getting my life in order. I'm confident, powerful, and, for once, would make my sisters proud."

"Baloney. You're running scared." Allegra froze. No one but Nate knew about Harry and his messages. How did Shirley know? "You're running as fast as you can from love. Have you seen Finn recently? He's been beating the crap out of everyone at Tigo's, and there was even a girl in his office when I left just now."

Allegra felt her heart clench. No matter how much she was finding herself and growing as a woman, she was always dreaming of Finn. Every night he came to her in her dreams. Every night she loved him with her whole heart the way she wanted to. And then morning came and she awoke alone.

"We have never been a couple."

"Well, this tramp certainly thought she was. What was her name?" Shirley looked up at the ceiling, and then her eyes dropped to look right at Allegra. "Oh yeah, Raven Eddie."

"What?" Allegra yelled.

Shirley couldn't hide her satisfied smile. "Oh, you know her?"

"Don't play innocent. You're no good at it." Shirley just shrugged and grinned. Allegra grabbed her purse. "Tell the driver to grab my bags. I'll meet him at the airport. And don't you dare think this means I'm going after Finn."

Allegra slammed the door on Shirley's laughter.

Finn looked at his watch and sighed quietly. Raven Eddie's father had threatened him within an inch of his life if he didn't have a meeting with her. Finally Finn had agreed to the meeting with the socialite. Why she needed an agent, he didn't know. She had been too busy hitting on him to tell him why she wanted to meet.

"Miss Eddie, please hop off my desk and tell me what you need."

Raven arched her back and pouted. Maybe she was here to be a porn star? That could be interesting. Instead of hopping off the desk, Raven spun around so she faced him. She crossed her legs slowly and Finn almost rolled his eyes. He didn't need to look to know she wasn't wearing panties.

Yep, porn star.

"I need an agent who can handle me. I was with Smithe Group, but they just didn't know what to do with me."

"Look, Miss Eddie, I'm late for my plane. We'll have to pick this up next week."

One leg arched over his head and caged him in. Finn confirmed the fact she wasn't wearing panties whether he wanted to or not.

"I want my own reality show."

Finn almost laughed, but when Raven ran her hands up his chest, the laughter turned into anger.

"As I live and breathe, is that you, Raven?"

Raven whipped around so fast she almost fell into Finn's lap. He leapt up and looked in wonder at Allegra. She was stunning in a tight, fitted pantsuit. Her legs looked a mile long in the red stilettos that matched the silk blouse. Her blond hair fell in soft curls around her shoulders and her makeup was flawless.

"Ah, there you are, sweetheart." Finn pleaded with his eyes for her to play along.

"Darling," Allegra cooed excitedly, "you didn't tell me you knew Raven. Did I ever tell you we went to high school together?"

Finn shook his head. So that was why she was here. Someone told her Raven was here. But, then why was she playing along? Finn kept his mouth shut as Allegra slowly walked behind the desk, lifted his chin with one perfectly manicured finger, and licked her red lips.

"I'm sorry I'm late. How will I ever make it up to you?" Finn felt his pulse quicken in response to her sultry question.

"You're dating Allegra Simpson?" Raven squeaked.

Finn looked down into Allegra's face and brushed back

a piece of hair. "She's always had my heart and always will. I'll call you if anything comes up, Raven, but Allegra and I have some unfinished business."

His heart wasn't the only thing pounding as his hand ran down Allegra's back. He heard Raven huff and then the door to the office slam. He didn't care. Right now Allegra was looking at him in a way he'd only dreamt of.

"What are you doing here, Allegra?"

"I heard Raven was here and thought you might need me."

"I always need you. Even when I try not to, I find myself needing you," Finn whispered. He felt her delicate hand tighten around his waist.

"Oh, Finn. What have I done? Am I too late? There's so much I need to tell you."

"Hey man, we need to go . . . Oh, sorry," Kane stopped as he walked into the room with his girlfriend and another model.

Finn cleared his throat. "Um, Allegra, you know Kane and Kelly, and this is Steffi."

Allegra took a step back. "Yes, I know. She's walked for me before."

"Hello, Miss Simpson," Steffi said in her German accent.

"I take it you'll be at Fashion Week. I'll see you there. I'm sorry, but my plane is waiting."

Allegra hurried from the room. "Allegra, wait!" Finn called, but she was already out the door. "Dammit!"

"I'm so sorry, man. I thought it was over," Kane said apologetically.

"I did, too. But if it wasn't before, it is now."

"Why don't you take my invitation to Simpson Fashion's party?" Kelly opened her purse and pulled out an embossed envelope. "I think you still have a chance. Only someone who cares would look that devastated. Fight for her, Finn."

"Won't you need this?"

Kelly laughed. "I'm a model, I can get in anywhere I want."

Finn grabbed the invitation like a lifeline. "Thank you. Now, let's get to New York. I have a woman to win back."

Allegra stepped into her family's condo in New York City and dropped her bag with relief. She had made it from the airport to her condo without anyone seeing the tears in her puffy, bloodshot eyes. She had to get over him. She had to forget him.

She wheeled her carry-on bag to her room where her suitcases waited to be unpacked. With a sigh, Allegra fell back onto the bed and stared up at the ceiling. She had messed up by not telling Finn the truth from the beginning, but she had been too scared to admit her weakness, too afraid to be lectured, too afraid to admit it was a problem, and too afraid to not be the perfect, nice one. Allegra felt as if she had just run a marathon. She was exhausted with grief and knowing it was all her fault that she pushed Finn away.

She shut her eyes, and before she knew it, she was asleep. Dark dreams filled her mind. Dreams of being watched, being judged, and being scolded in harsh whispers. Dreams of a touch she didn't want—a hand trailing down her arm before disappearing into the mist of her dream, leaving behind a smell of cologne that wasn't Finn's. Knowing it would never be Finn's, her heart broke all over again.

Allegra's eyes shot open. Tears had filled them, and as she took a deep breath to calm herself in the room gone dark with night, she breathed in the cologne from her dreams.

"Great, now I'm really going crazy." Allegra shook her head to clear the fog and looked at the clock. Eight-thirty. Crap! She bolted from the bed and ripped open her suitcases.

She hurried to hang her clothes in the closet and stripped naked. She had to meet David and Josh from Bellerose in thirty minutes. Grabbing some perfume, she spritzed herself in lieu of a shower. She struggled to get on a pair of the tightest skinny jeans she owned. Jumping to the bed with the pants stuck at her knees, she fell onto the bed and started wiggling her hips. She contemplated calling the maintenance man to bring some pliers when she finally got them over her hips. Sucking in her tummy for all she was worth, she managed to get the damn jeans buttoned.

Struggling to sit up, she opted to roll off the bed and onto the floor where she crawled to the closet, pulled herself up, and breathed for the first time. God, she couldn't wait for these jeans to go out of fashion. She grabbed a loose caramel-colored sweater and brown leather knee-high boots. Her perfectly blown-out hair was smashed on one side and sticking out the other. Opting for casual elegance, she whipped it into a loose bun and swiped on some clear lip gloss before doing lunges out her door in hopes of loosening her jeans.

Finn sat at dinner with the head of the advertising department for a deodorant company. He was going on and on about Kane starring in the commercial tomorrow. Finn should be excited; it was a great opportunity for Kane and for Simpson Entertainment Agency. But all he could think about was Allegra's face full of pain as she ran from his office earlier that day.

Finn set his napkin down and pulled out his phone. Nine o'clock. This meeting was lasting forever. A sudden feeling akin to panic filled his body. He needed to get to her. He needed to get to her now to explain how he felt. He needed to beg her to take a chance on a washed-up ballplayer from the wrong side of the tracks.

"I'm sorry, I'm being called away on more business. Kane can take it from here. I'll see you on set in the morning."

Finn pushed his long legs back and stood up. He reached over the table and shook the hand of the advertising exec before shooting Kane a look of pure determination. Kane smiled back, and Finn knew he understood.

He strode from the restaurant with more determination than a player at the bottom of the ninth, needing a home run to win the game. He was not a quitter, and he was going to fight for the woman he loved.

Chapter Five

"What do you mean she's not in?" Finn said angrily to the doorman at Allegra's condo.

"She left just a little while ago for a dinner meeting. I'm sorry, Mr. Williams. She's not here, and I can't let you in her condo to wait. You can wait in the lobby if you'd like," the man said without a hint of remorse. Didn't he know how desperate Finn was to see her?

Finn ran a hand over his short, neatly trimmed black hair and let out a long-suffering breath. The doorman's face softened and he cleared his throat. "I don't know how long she'll be at François. Could be for another hour or two."

Finn's head shot up. "Thanks, man!" Finn shot from the lobby and whistled for the first taxi he could find. He had a woman to find . . . *his* woman.

Allegra got out of her private car and looked at the glowing restaurant. She couldn't shake the feeling someone was watching her. Ever since her dream, she'd felt dirty. She looked around slowly and took in the streets of SoHo. The lights cast a yellow glow on the gray cement sidewalks. Shadows stretched liked fingers between the buildings, edging a step closer to the brightly lit restaurant.

Allegra blinked a couple of times. She would have sworn a shadow moved, but then the hair on the back of her neck stood up and she whipped around. Across the street—was that man watching her?

"OMG! We're totally late," Josh Rose yelled as he waved his hand at her. He and his partner, David Bell, got out of a car and hurried toward her. "I'm so sorry, we got stuck on site and didn't realize how late it was. But the good news is the set looks amazing. The runway is beyond dramatic."

David smiled at his more exuberant other half and leaned forward to kiss Allegra's cheek. "It's good to see you again. You're going to love the show tomorrow."

The shadows were forgotten in the bright light of Josh and David's smiles. Allegra clasped their hands and walked with them into François for dinner. "I can't wait to see it. I saw the mock-ups of the set, and they are breathtaking. Are you really having the models walk through a waterfall of crystals? Aren't you worried they'll fall?"

Allegra, Josh, and David sat down at the table and ordered a bottle of champagne. "Honey, I've had these girls practicing since we cast them last week. They know if they fall they won't have a prayer of being picked up to walk at Milan or Paris. That will keep their stilettos sure and steady," Josh told her with certainty.

"Well, I think the jewels theme is fantastic. Your clothes are amazing as always." Allegra smiled as they toasted.

"What about your show?" David asked. "I saw it on the schedule. You're hosting it on Wall Street?"

Allegra smiled. It had taken a lot to talk the city into allowing her to shut down a block of the street outside the business district. "It's just a small show—simple elegance for working women during the day and party attire for night. It's a small line, but a luxurious one. I have men lining the runway in business suits and briefcases. The women will strip off their jackets revealing outfits for nighttime attire. It should be perfect with the hustle and bustle of the town surrounding them."

"Well, we will be there. Tomorrow afternoon, right?

"One o'clock."

"Perfect. We'll see your show, then go to ours that evening. What other shows are you going to?" David asked.

"I have six houses putting on shows. Montclaire, you guys, and Lux4U, to name a few. I finish up on Friday, and the Simpson Fashion party will be at the NITE club that evening."

"Oh, I can't wait. Isn't that the club owned by that super-hot actor . . .?" Josh snapped his fingers trying to think of the name.

"Nate Reece," David reminded him.

Allegra grinned and nodded. "He's part owner, and he'll be there."

"Lawdy! If we could get him to appear in a Bellerose campaign . . ." Josh said wistfully.

"Why don't you ask him when you see him at the party? We went to high school together."

David leaned forward seriously. "Tell us everything we need to know to get him to agree."

Finn leapt from the taxi and pushed past the line waiting for a table at François. The small restaurant was filled with people and he scanned the crowd, looking for Allegra.

"Can I help you, sir?" the maître d' asked.

"Yes, I'm meeting Allegra Simpson here. I'm afraid I'm rather late."

"Her party was only for three. Are you sure it was tonight?"

"Yes. I'm not eating. Just meeting her party before

heading to another appointment," Finn said in the most annoyed way he could. Growing up, his mother would have smacked the back of his head for talking like this. But being around powerful people had taught Finn a thing or two about bored annoyance. It seemed to make people feel more important.

"Of course. This way." The maître d' led him around the room to a table in the back. He saw her then, laughing with David and Josh.

Josh was the first to see him. "Finn! What a pleasant surprise. Have you decided to take us up on our offer to model for us?"

Finn relaxed. Dinner with David and Josh was way different from dinner with men more interested on hitting on her than on business. "Sorry, gentlemen. I'm here for Allegra."

Allegra's blue eyes widened as she looked silently at him. He could see the emotions running across her face—anger, hope, and something else that gave him the courage to reach out and take her hands in his.

"Allegra, I've been a complete fool. I know something has been wrong, and I was more worried about trying to impress you than doing what I should have done in the first place—be there for you. We started off as friends, but then it grew into something more. At least it did for me. Your presence lights my soul, and I can't imagine not having you in my life. Please say you'll forgive me. Please tell me I wasn't imagining that you have feelings for me. And if I was, then forget this whole thing and take me as your friend. I'd rather have you in my life as a friend than to lose you completely."

Sniff. Josh dabbed his eyes and David smiled at Finn.

Allegra didn't move. She couldn't. His words were floating around her head as if in a dream. As if it were a wonderful dream. Would it all end when she woke up?

"Is this a dream?"

Finn chuckled and brought her hands up to his lips for a soft kiss. "No. Please say you'll give me a chance. I know I'm not part of the country club scene. I know I grew up in one of the worst neighborhoods in Atlanta. I know they'll say I'm not good enough for you. But I will fight for your love every day. I will never stop trying to love you more."

Allegra felt a tear silently escape and roll down her cheek before she threw her arms around Finn's neck. "I've been so stupid, Finn. I'm so sorry. It's me who needs to fight to deserve you."

"Gentlemen, if you would excuse us. I'd like to take Allegra home," Finn said, his eyes never leaving Allegra's.

"By all means. We'll see you tomorrow at your show. We're so happy for you both," David said as he and Josh hurried from the restaurant. By morning everyone would know about Finn's romantic speech.

"You love me?" Allegra asked as soon as he closed the door to the private car. The privacy divider went up, and Finn kissed her in response to her question. His lips were soft and warm. His fingers threaded into her hair as he angled her head to kiss her more firmly. The kiss went from soft and gentle to hard and wild in a split second.

Tongues caressed, fingers gripped, and moans echoed in the back of the car. They kissed desperately, both knowing they had nearly missed their chance. Allegra's head fell back as Finn tore his mouth from hers and trailed kisses down her neck. His hot lips burnt a path down to the V of her collarbone and nipped at her taunt nipple through her sweater.

Allegra pushed at his coat, desperate to see him. "Allegra," Finn groaned. "We can't."

"Why not?" She gasped as she fought to undress him.

"Because we're at your place. We have to get out of the car."

Allegra pulled back quickly. "Why didn't you say so? Hurry up. The faster we get upstairs, the faster I can have you naked."

Finn tossed his head back and laughed. "It looks like someone has learned to speak her mind."

Allegra bit down nervously on her lip. "Does that bother you?"

"Hell no." Finn leaned forward, his lips brushing the sensitive shell of her ear as he whispered, "Tell me more of what you want me to do to you."

Allegra's face turned five shades of red. She couldn't, could she? "I want you to . . ." Allegra paused. *Have sex with me? That was kind of boring. Make love to me? He did say he loved me, but was that as sexy as something down and dirty like bang me against a wall? Ow, bang sounded like it would hurt. Fuc – oh no, a Southern lady couldn't say that. Umm, put your penis in my vagina? No, too technical. Let's shag? Too British. Spread my dewy petals and spear me with your manroot? No, too historical romance novel.* Allegra was saved when the car door opened.

Finn stood and held out his hand for her. Fiddlesticks, she had to think of something sexy to say before they reached her condo. *I want to lick the ridges of your six-pack? Ugh!* Now she sounded like a poodle. This was horrible. Allegra felt her shoulders slump in defeat.

"Hey, are you okay? We don't have to do anything if you don't want to," Finn said quietly as the doors to the elevator closed.

"It's not that, it's just . . . well, I'm not sexy. I can't talk dirty. I don't know how to twerk. And I don't even own a vibrator. I'm a sexual dunce," Allegra confessed. She was sure Finn would escort her off the elevator and then run for the stairs. What she didn't expect was the wide grin on his face. "What?"

"Sweetheart, you're delirious if you think you aren't sexy. You're breathtaking. Do you know how hard it is to control myself around you? Did you really think that when I make love to you I'd make you do a strip tease and pleasure yourself with a dildo? I'd be insulted. The only thing I want inside you is me."

Allegra felt fire spread to her face and then shoot straight to her core. Vapors weren't caused from the Southern heat. No, sexy gentlemen saying things like that caused vapors.

"Okay," Allegra forced out as she stared at the growing erection in his pants. Yep, that's what caused vapors all right.

Finn was having a very hard time not pushing Allegra against the wall of the elevator and having his way with her right then and there. He had to close his eyes and run baseball stats through his mind when she unconsciously licked her lips as she stared at his erection. Not sexy? This woman was the definition of sexy. Mostly because she didn't try to be sexy.

The doors to the elevator slid quietly open, and she stepped out hesitantly. She eyed him as if she thought he'd bolt. Didn't she know that no power in this world would drag him away from her tonight?

"Here." Finn took the keys from her hand and unlocked

the door.

This was the first time he'd been in the Simpsons' New York condo. He glanced around at the living room surrounded on three sides by floor-to-ceiling windows. He saw a bit of the state-of-the-art kitchen and the hall leading to the bedrooms. No matter how much this penthouse cost, it made him feel comfortable. There were family pictures on the walls, not priceless works of art. Comfortable couches filled the living room. A pair of bunny slippers sat under a coffee table full of magazines.

Allegra set her purse down and moved to the large windows overlooking the city. They didn't need to turn on a light; the glow of the city lit the room like a million candles. Finn shrugged out of his suit coat and tossed it over a chair. He slowly walked to where she stood nervously. He had every intention of showing Allegra just how sexy he found her.

He stopped behind her and gently laid his hand at the base of her neck. His thumb moved slowly up and down her soft skin; Allegra automatically tilted her head forward, enjoying his sensual neck massage. Finn had to concentrate on breathing. It would be so easy to forget. But as he took a step closer to her and felt the curve of her bottom brush against his thighs, he decided breathing was overrated.

Finn looked out the window at the luminous city below. Thousands of red and white car lights twinkled like stars below them. The soft curve of her neck drew his attention away from the city. He bent his head and lowered his lips to the back of her neck. She pushed against him instinctually, and Finn dropped his hands to grip her hips. His fingers flexed as he pulled her tightly against him. His lips moved from one spot to the next as he kissed his way down her neck.

Allegra moaned softly and Finn had to remind himself to take it slow. He reached for her sweater and slid his hands underneath it. His thumbs skimmed across her flat stomach, and Allegra pressed her bottom more firmly against his erection, causing it to jump in eager anticipation.

As he sucked in the delicate skin at the base of her neck, Finn explored her rib cage until his thumbs brushed the underside of her lace-covered breasts. God, they were perfect. His hands covered them, and he lightly squeezed them before running his thumbs over her pebbled nipples. Allegra tossed her head back against his shoulder as Finn teased her. He watched her face in the reflection of the windows. She may not realize it, but her closed eyes and her mouth slightly open in pleasure were the sexiest images he'd ever seen.

Reaching down, he pulled her sweater up and over her head. When she went to turn to face him, he held her in place. He wanted to see every reaction she had to him. He unclasped her bra and let it fall to the floor. In the windows, he saw the reflection of her breasts. He moved his hands to cover them, to explore them, and to love them. When Allegra writhed against him, Finn slid his hand to the waist of her jeans and unbuttoned them.

It took both of them a minute to peel them off her, but when she bent against him he nearly exploded as she shook her hips as to shimmy out of them. As soon as she stepped free of the jeans, Finn pulled her against him again. He had to feel her. He cupped her breasts again and watched his hands play with her nipples in the reflection. As she moaned his name, he watched and moved one hand down her stomach. He'd never seen anything so erotic as when his hand disappeared beneath her matching lace panties.

Allegra's head was thrown back, and her eyes squeezed shut. Finn's fingers slid into her; Allegra's body flushed with heat, her stomach plummeted, and then she exploded.

"Finn," she gasped and clutched his muscled forearm. His hand dropped from her breast and wrapped around her waist, holding her up as she came.

When she opened her eyes, she saw his reflection in the window. The look of pure desire on his strong face had her heart thumping wildly.

"Now you know how sexy you are. You amaze me," he whispered in her ear as his hands cupped her swollen breasts again. "I love you, Allegra. All of you."

Allegra turned in his arms. She leaned her head back to see his face; he'd given her the courage to do what she wanted now. If she could run her own company, she sure as hell could tell the man she loved what she wanted.

"Finn, I think we need to get you undressed."

"Yes, ma'am." Finn grinned as he unbuttoned his dress shirt and let it drop to the floor along with his pants. Allegra took a long, slow gaze. His chest was wide with corded muscles wrapping around his tall body. His waist narrowed slightly and his muscles formed a V pointing right to a very impressive, very large erection.

Finn drew her attention away from his body when he ran his fingers through her hair and looked into her eyes. Allegra felt her hair fall around her bare shoulders as their lips met, and he backed her up until she gasped into his mouth as her bottom met the cool glass.

"What do you want, Allegra?"

"You." It was all she had to say. Finn's whole body reacted, and Allegra shivered in anticipation.

He didn't break from their kiss as he sheathed himself with a condom. He didn't break the kiss when he ran his hands down her sides, over her hips, and grabbed the back of her legs, wrapping them around his waist, pushing her against the window. And he didn't break the kiss as he filled her completely.

Allegra gasped as he moved in and out of her, driving her closer and closer to the edge. The lights from the city blurred as her body convulsed around Finn. He shouted her name as he thrust one last time into her and stilled.

"Never doubt how sexy you are to me. I want you this much no matter the time of day or what you're wearing."

"Finn?"

"Yes?"

Allegra felt her lips quirk. "I love you, too. Now shut up and take me to bed."

Finn moved his other hand to cup her bottom and smiled. "Anything for you, Allegra," he said as he carried her down the hall.

Chapter Six

Finn walked back into the bedroom as the early morning sunlight filled the room. It had killed him to get out of bed, but if he didn't hurry he would be late for Kane's commercial shoot. Bending over, he kissed Allegra gently on the lips.

"I have to go, sweetheart."

"Do you have to?" Allegra mumbled sleepily.

"I do. And I bet you have to get going, too. Your house walks later today. I'll do everything I can to get there to see it. I know everyone will love it."

Allegra's eyes flew open. "Oh my gosh, my show!" Allegra leapt from bed naked and then skidded to a stop halfway across the room before turning around and hurrying back to press a lingering kiss on his lips. He didn't want to leave her today, but the real world was knocking loudly. Literally.

"I'll leave a ticket for you. Would you mind getting the door on your way out?"

"Of course. I love you."

"I love you."

Finn watched Allegra hurry into the bathroom and shut the door. He walked through the condo and opened the door for one of the desk clerks.

"Oh, um, Miss Simpson has a delivery." The young

man shoved a huge bouquet of flowers at Finn.

"Thank you." Finn carried the white roses into the living room and set them on the table. He was sure someone was sending them to wish her luck for the fashion show. Maybe he should do something like that for her, too, he thought as he locked the front door behind him.

Allegra smiled to herself and hummed as she started the shower. As the water heated up, she walked into her closet to pull out a black bra and panties set. She felt sexy today and wanted to feel it from the inside out. Looking around her closet, she picked out the sexiest of her collection, a skintight scarlet-red dress with a plunging neckline. With a fitted jacket over it, it would be perfect. She laid it out the bed and then stepped into the shower.

The hot water trickled down her body as she remembered all the things she and Finn had done the night before. She was so happy she didn't think she could stand it. After all this time of wanting and longing, she finally had a love she didn't think she'd ever have, and she wanted to shout it from the rooftop.

Allegra heard the faint sound of the door to her condo clicking shut and paused. She wiped her hand across the steamy shower glass and looked out. "Did you forget something?" Allegra called out. She paused, waiting to hear Finn's answer, but none came. "Finn?"

Allegra opened the glass shower door and stuck her head out so she could hear. "Finn?"

Straining her ears, all Allegra heard was the shower. She laughed to herself and went back to washing her hair and humming. Enough foolishness. Harry was in Atlanta, and she needed to focus on the fashion show happening in four hours. Her own line was small, just a hobby really. But she loved creating things for the everyday woman. So many of the shows at fashion weeks around the world were so impractical. Garbage bags made into haute couture, models walking with their heads in cones that resemble something a dog would wear after being neutered—the list went on and on. Instead of something only size double zero models could wear, Allegra designed clothes she would wear. Everyone deserved to feel the magic of well-designed clothes.

Allegra turned off the water and stepped out of the shower to towel off. She brushed her wet hair and wrapped the towel around her breasts before padding out to her bedroom.

She stopped as soon as she entered her room. Everything was in place, but something was different. What was it? As she looked around, her body broke out in goose bumps. Adrenaline pumped through her as she stepped farther into the room. Her door was open, just like Finn had left it. Her red dress lay on her bed next to her white bra and panties . . . Allegra froze and stared down at the bed. Hadn't she picked out black underwear? But lying exactly where she had placed her black bra and panties lay a pair of white ones. With a shaky hand she reached out and picked them up. They were hers. Did she switch them? Did Finn come back in and switch them? She was so worked up about her fashion show she couldn't remember. It might be embarrassing, but she'd call Finn and find out if he'd done it.

Looking around, she remembered her phone was in her purse by the door. Gripping her bra and panties in one hand and her towel in the other, she walked into the living room. She saw the flowers and smiled. Finn was so sweet. How did she get so lucky?

Picking up her purse, she dug out her phone and called Finn. "Hello. You've reached Finn Williams, Vice President of Simpson Entertainment . . ."

Allegra hung up the phone without leaving a message. He would be busy with Kane's commercial. It's foolish anyway. She was sure she changed them out without realizing it. She was in such an orgasm-induced state anyway, she practically forgot her own fashion show.

As she headed back to her room, she looked back at the flowers. A card stuck out the side. She wondered if Finn had written something sweet or something naughty to her. Allegra grinned with anticipation as she reached for the red envelope and pulled out the white card. She turned it over. There was only one word written on it . . . *Whore*.

Allegra felt her knees give out as she collapsed on the floor. He was here. Harry was here. Clutching the phone, she struggled to enter her passcode. Her fingers shook and she kept hitting the wrong buttons. With every wrong number, she felt her vision blur. She struggled to breathe. Finally she entered the right numbers and called the only person who knew the truth.

"Damien, he's here. He's in New York."

Finn clutched his hand as the director yelled, "Cut!"

This was take one hundred if Finn had been counting right. He looked at his watch. Allegra's show was starting at any moment, and he was going to miss it because this guy thought a commercial was supposed to be artistic. What the hell does artistic have to do with deodorant?

"Man, can I just bail on this?" Kane whispered.

"Not unless you're prepared to pay them a couple

million dollars. Remember, you're making seven million off this."

"But really? What the hell? He wants me to wear this?" Kane held out the white pirate shirt and kilt.

"Highlanders are big right now."

"My ancestors are from Africa, not Scotland. And he does know that Highlanders didn't wear kilts on pirate ships while speaking with an American accent, right?" Kane said through gritted teeth.

"Okay!" the director called through the bullhorn. "Let's have Kane swing on the rope across the deck and into the arms of the wenches again."

"Wenches, Finn, wenches . . . on a pirate ship."

"Seven million dollars, Kane." Finn laughed. This will make a great story for Allegra. He couldn't wait to see her and tell her all about it.

Allegra threw herself into the chaos of the dressing room behind the scenes of her fashion show. Wall Street was packed with people to see her show, but no Finn. Damien was investigating the flower delivery and in the meantime had sent some of New York's finest off-duty SWAT officers to stand guard. They tried to hide their smiles as they watched models ripping off their clothes and yelling at their dressers to hurry.

At least she felt safe for now. One of the officers was going to accompany her as her driver wherever she went. Allegra couldn't decide which she wanted—for Harry to make a move and be caught or to be scared away.

"Angelica, go," Allegra hissed to one of the models. The model's eyes narrowed as she walked around the curtain and strutted down the runway. Allegra watched on the TV screen as Angelica stopped at the end of the runway and posed before spinning on her toes and heading back up the runway past Kelly, Kane's girlfriend, as she closed out the show in Allegra's favorite dress.

"That's it, ladies! Line up for the final walk." Allegra stepped back as all the women got in order behind the curtain. As soon as Kelly was out of sight of the audience, she ran around the corner to get in front of Allegra.

"So, about what you saw at the office," Kelly started to say as the models began their last runway walk as a group.

"It's okay, Kelly. Finn and I worked it out," Allegra said with a blush. They'd worked it out in lots of ways last night. Allegra rolled her eyes at herself. See, sexual dunce. She couldn't even make a sexual innuendo to herself without it sounding corny.

Kelly grinned as if she could read her mind, but the second before she stepped around the curtain, the smile dropped, and she transformed before strutting down the runway to the resounding cheers of the audience. Allegra took a deep breath and counted to ten before stepping out from behind the curtain. She saw David and Josh standing and cheering. She scanned the crowd but didn't see Finn. She also breathed a sigh of relief when she didn't see Harry either. The models finally smiled and clapped as Allegra walked down the runway waving and smiling. She'd done it—all by herself. She was woman, and she'd just roared without saying a word.

"Ma'am, wait here please," the officer said as he held up a hand. Allegra was in a hurry, but stood in the hallway as the officer went into her apartment. She had less than an hour to get changed and over to Bellerose's show. Hopefully, this officer had one of those little flashing lights he could put on the roof of the car he was driving for her.

Allegra took a deep breath and pulled out her phone to watch the minutes tick by. What was taking him so long? Her phone beeped, and she saw a message from Finn that the commercial had just now wrapped. Allegra typed in the address of the Bellerose show and told him to wear the nicest suit he had. Where her show was pretty laid back in terms of theatrics, Bellerose was going to the max.

"Okay, all clear."

Allegra rushed past the officer and slammed the door to her bedroom. She was stripped out of her clothes before she even reached the closet. She grabbed the black lace mini dress David and Josh had designed for her before wedging her feet into six-inch hot pink stiletto boots fashioned to look like a rose blossom.

Rushing out of the closet, Allegra tried not to fall as she leapt into the bathroom to redo her hair and makeup. She heard the doorbell and the officer answering it. Since he didn't come get her, she figured it wasn't important and hurried to grab her small clutch before running—more like tippy-toe dancing—her way down the hall as fast as she could.

"Let's go," she called before slamming into the back of the officer. "What? Come on!" But then Allegra looked around him at the single white rose on her coffee table with a red envelope next to it.

"This just arrived. I have officers talking to the doorman. I think you better stay here."

Allegra was in too much of a hurry to be scared. "Then he would win. This is a huge fashion show. I can't miss it." Allegra grabbed the envelope and ripped it open. "Well, at least he can say more than one word now."

You're mine and mine alone. Always mine, Allegra.

"That implies you were his at one time. Officers are on

their way and your Secret Service buddy has been called."

"I already know who it is. Harry Daniels. I've told you all this before."

"Yes, but we can't find him. And we have to make sure it's not someone else."

Allegra opened the door and made shooing motions with her hands. "Come on. You can quiz me all about it in the car. Do you have a siren?"

He smiled into the shadows as he watched his wife run out the front door of her building. He watched her all the time and knew the look on her face. She had received his gift. Pride swelled in his heart. He'd given his wife a gift, and she loved it. He could tell. Her driver hurried to open the door before she did. Oh, she was beautiful tonight. Although that skirt was a bit short. What a filthy whore she was. She was supposed to wear things like that for him and him alone. Anger and excitement pulsed through his body. She would learn soon enough that no one rejected him. No one, especially his soon-to-be wife.

"Soon, Allegra, soon."

Finn found the annoyed assistant with a headpiece standing outside the door to the Bellerose show. "Finn Williams?"

"That's me," Finn said with a smile. This guy couldn't be more than five and a half feet tall. A wet dishrag probably weighed more, but the cold indifferent stare on his face had Finn alternately laughing and respecting him. This guy wouldn't be a pushover.

"Here's your ticket; let me take you to your seat. The show starts in a few minutes."

"Is Allegra here yet?"

"No," the assistant said in a huff. "But these parent house types are always like that. She'll probably get here ten seconds before the show starts. They're *so* dramatic."

Finn covered his laugh with a cough and followed the man to a seat in the front row. The man gave a curt nod and hurried back out front, presumably to wait for Allegra.

He took his seat and ignored the giggling actress next to him. "Hey, man. Don't I know you?" Finn looked around the actress to the man he had seen hugging Allegra weeks ago. "That's right. You know Leggy."

Finn felt his blood boil. He'd always been a relaxed dater. If things worked, great. If not, great. He was never overprotective. He never felt he had to be. Women usually fought to be with him, but now he felt it—jealousy. It was new to him and he didn't like it. The thought of this guy knowing Allegra so well made him want to pummel the guy.

"Yes, I know her . . . *very* well."

The man's smile just widened in response to Finn.

"Yeah, so do I. Nate Reece." The man held out his hand, and Finn shook it automatically.

"Finn Williams."

"Baby, stop talking to this nobody. There's the photographer for *Vogue*," the woman whined.

Finn watched as Nate's hand went to her knee, his arm wrapped around her shoulder, and he leaned in to whisper in her ear. The actress blushed and laughed. This guy was a womanizer if he ever saw one, and now he was asking about Allegra. Finn gritted his teeth as his mind went in directions he didn't want it to go.

"I'm so sorry I'm late," Allegra whispered in his ear, causing him to jump.

"Where did you come from?"

"Backstage. I wanted to wish David and Josh good luck. I missed you." Allegra leaned over and kissed him. His anger disappeared and neither the lights dimming, the crystal waterfall flowing, nor the models stomping by could draw his attention from the woman next to him.

"I'm so glad you're here. I was stuck talking to your ex-boyfriend. I can see why you broke up with him." Finn was taken aback at how fast Allegra changed. Sure, he shouldn't bad-mouth someone she'd dated, but he wasn't expecting her to go white and her grasp to tighten on his hand.

"Harry?" she gasped as she looked around.

"No, Nate Reece," Finn told her. Color rushed back to her face and her hand loosened its grip.

"Oh, Nate!" Allegra leaned forward and waved. Finn clutched his jaw when the bastard blew her a kiss. "He's great, isn't he?"

"Dandy."

Allegra's eyes widened in surprise. "Well, yes, but how did you know?"

"What?"

"Oh," Allegra laughed, "nothing."

"Wait, who's Harry?"

Finn saw the reaction immediately. She lost her glow. "He's who I've needed to talk to you about. He's the reason I couldn't tell you how I felt. But, it's a talk for another time . . . tonight, when we get home."

Finn wrapped his arm around her and felt her nuzzle in closer to him. Nate Reece could kiss his ass. He had Allegra now, and he'd never let her go. Ever.

Chapter Seven

Allegra stood up and cheered as David and Josh walked the runway with their models. They'd done it. Their show had been astonishing. She watched as editors and advertisers typed feverishly, posted pictures, emailed offers to the models, and ordered Bellerose clothing.

Finn stood stiffly next to her as Nate made his way over and kissed her cheek.

"Oh my God, what a hunk," Nate whispered in her ear and Allegra tried to hide her laugh.

"I know." She was sure the press was writing it up that Nate was hitting on her in front of her boyfriend.

"How's the other problem?"

Allegra felt her face tighten into a forced smile. "He's here."

"Did you call the cops? What does Finn say about it?"

"There's security right behind me pretending to be my driver. I'm telling Finn about it tonight."

"You need to tell him," was all Finn heard Nate whisper into Allegra's ear. What was going on? Was Nate making his move? Finn felt his heart tighten in his chest. He was about to lose the best thing to ever happen to him.

"Come on, sweetheart. Let's go congratulate the guys."

Nate smiled at them both. "Tell them it was a great show. I'll meet with them at the after-party. Tell them to bring their best offer." Nate kissed her cheek. "Call me if you need me—anytime. Promise?"

"Promise." Allegra smiled kindly as she squeezed his hand. Finn knew he was bordering on acting like a toddler in the middle of a tantrum, but he didn't care. He pulled Allegra away.

"Did you enjoy the show?" he asked.

"I'm so proud of them. They outdid themselves. But, Finn, I only want to stay for a little while. There are things we need to talk about."

Finn nodded. He couldn't speak. He knew what she was going to say. She was choosing Nate Reece.

Finn sat back against the leather seat and closed his eyes. Allegra had been different all night. She'd been flustered, fake, and distracted. She was avoiding something—most likely him. When he heard the partition rise, he knew the speech was coming.

"Go ahead. Say it," Finn challenged her without opening his eyes.

"I have this ex-boyfriend," Allegra started to say before taking a deep breath. "He won't leave me alone."

Finn's eyes flew open, and he sat up in his seat. "Nate won't leave you alone? I'll kick his ass."

"No, Finn. It's not Nate. I dated this guy named Harry Daniels. I met him online. When I met him in person he wasn't anything like he was online, but I thought he was funny so I gave him a chance. We started dating and things were fine until we, um, had sex."

Finn swallowed the comment he was going to say. Allegra was clearly upset. She had started to shake. He needed to be supportive, not jealous and obsessive. "Go on, sweetheart." He wrapped his arm around her, and she laid her head on his chest. He'd protect her. He'd take care of her. No matter what this asshole did.

"He started slowly—telling me I was stupid, telling me I couldn't do anything myself. That it was good he was there to tell me what to do or I'd likely kill myself. He said I was horrible in bed. I wasn't sexy. I wasn't even pretty. I became so self-conscious about everything I did, from what I wore, to my own designs, and even wondering if I was ordering pizza right." Allegra let out a long breath. "I finally broke up with him. My sisters all said *I told you so.* They had been trying to get me to break up with him for months. So, my confidence couldn't handle it when he started to stalk me. I was scared to go to my sisters. Between him and their *I told you so*'s, I felt worthless and stupid."

"What did you do?"

"Nothing at first. But then I tried to meet with him and tell him it wasn't going to happen. I told him we could be friends. All the usual lines."

Finn held back his comment about her being too nice. Her sisters had been right about that. He'd heard Elle talk to Bree about it many times. They worried she wouldn't be able to stand up for herself. It was one of the reasons Finn had asked her if she wanted to join him to work out in the mornings. That, and he wanted to be near her.

"About six months after we broke up and I had that talk with him, everything got better. He hadn't called, hadn't emailed, and no longer stopped by my house. I thought he'd moved on. That's when you and I started going to the gym together and, um, working together more. It's when I started falling for you. But then I started getting these anonymous texts and emails threatening me."

"How were they threatening?"

"They said I was his and his alone. That I was a whore if I looked at another man, and he'd have to punish me if I left him. I was afraid of what he'd do. I was afraid he'd hurt you."

Finn fought the anger coursing through him and ran a gentle hand over her hair instead. She needed his support. "One asshole isn't going to scare me away. I love you too much to just walk away." This jackass had no idea the type of man Finn was—what he'd done, seen, and was prepared to do to keep the woman he loved safe.

"I'm so sorry I didn't tell you before. I was embarrassed I couldn't handle it on my own. I confronted Harry a month ago, and things have been quiet. But those flowers that were delivered to me this morning, they were from him. He called me a whore. He must have known you were with me. And then today, I received another note reminding me I was his. Somehow he knows I've moved on, and now I'm scared he'll do something rash."

"Have you called the police?"

"Yes. That's actually an off-duty SWAT officer driving the car. And I called Damien. He's trying to track down who sent the flowers and is working with the Georgia state troopers to find Harry. So far they haven't found him or his car. All his information has been handed over to the police up here."

"What about Mallory? Why isn't she here or someone from her firm?" Finn asked. Mallory Westin was Elle's best friend and basically another sister to Allegra. She was a socialite-turned-security expert and would fit in perfectly at Fashion Week.

"I haven't told anyone in my family. I just can't. I'm

tired of the pathetic looks and being treated like a baby."

"Okay. I won't tell them, but I'm glad you trusted me enough to tell me. Kane wrapped up his commercial shoot today. All I have are some meetings over the next couple of days, but I'm free every night. I don't want you alone until this guy is caught."

"I won't be. I'll have the protection detail. Thank you for listening and not telling me I handled this all wrong. I know I did. I should have filed a restraining order after the first email, but I was so embarrassed."

Finn knew how much Allegra liked to please people. She was the one who always brought peace to the bickering siblings or the one who smoothed over upset investors. She was the nice one. Elle was the bossy one, Bree was the scary one, and Reid was the laid-back one. Although, he'd learned, it was always the nice ones you had to look out for. You never expected their bite.

"Is that why you went to Tigo's every morning?"

"You knew about that?"

Finn chuckled. "I introduced your family to my gym in the bad part of town. Don't you think I'd know if you were still going there? Tigo told me."

"It was so cool. He taught me all this self-defense."

"Good. That was really smart of you to do. There's a time to be nice, and then there's a time to fight for your life."

"I'll remember that. I'm determined to move on with my life. He almost made me lose you once, but never again."

The car came to a stop, and the officer opened the door for them. "Don't worry, I have plenty of ideas on how we can take your mind off him," Finn whispered as they made their way to her condo.

His fingers dug so deeply into the palms of his hands he felt the warmth of his own blood dripping to the concrete sidewalk. He watched Allegra lay her head on that man's shoulder and disappear through the lobby. She didn't take his warnings seriously. Well, he'd show her. She'd be begging him to forgive her by the time he was done with her.

Allegra lay in bed as she watched Finn get ready for the day. The past two days had flown by, and tonight was her party. It was also the day Finn was the busiest. He was meeting with two companies interested in hiring Kane to be their spokesperson. She had two fashion shows to attend and then would be running over to NITE to make sure it was ready for the crush of people she was expecting for her after-party.

She'd get going soon enough, but she was really enjoying the view. Finn wasn't self-conscious at all as he walked around naked. He sat at the end of the bed and slid his shirt over his head. "I got you something today. To celebrate with tonight."

Allegra sat up, letting the sheet fall from her bare breasts and pool in her lap. "Really? What did you get me?"

"It's a surprise. But it's for tonight after we get home."

"When do I get it?" Allegra asked excitedly. She was a sucker for gifts.

"When I decide it's the right time. Besides, you're cute when you're this excited." Finn stepped into his pants and tucked in his shirt.

"Fine," Allegra teasingly whined. "I'm going to take my shower. I have my last shows, and then I'll come back here to change for the party. Will I see you here or at the party?"

"Probably at the party. Keep the officer with you. I know it's been quiet, but Damien said they haven't found Harry yet. You shouldn't take any chances."

"I won't. Now come kiss me goodbye."

"I think I can manage that." Finn smiled as he crawled up the bed. He didn't stop until his hands were beside her head and his hips were pressed against hers.

He lowered his head and captured her lips in a kiss meant to leave her desperate for more. Then he pulled away and smiled down at her. "Have a great day. I love you."

"Uh!" Allegra threw a pillow at him. "You leave me in a state like this and tell me to have a good day?"

Finn laughed as he headed out the door.

He waited as the bastard left his condo. That was *his* home with *his* wife. Why did he want to marry such a whore? But he'd teach her. He'd been planning their marriage since before they even met. He'd seen her pictures online and knew she was the one. *His*. Then he met her, and he knew he'd chosen wisely. She'd submit to him. She'd beg him. He'd had their whole life planned out when she rejected him, and this trash moved in on him.

He thought he'd won her back when he sent her those emails and texts. And she had stopped seeing Finn, just as he knew she would. She *submitted*. But just like every good woman, she needed to be broken. He looked down at the white box he held in his hands. It was the first of her lessons.

The doorman closed the door, but he didn't need to go in the front. He walked along the side of the building and waited. Sure enough, the building super was coming in and out carrying supplies. He waited until the supervisor turned his back and walked right in the side door and pressed the button to the penthouse.

Stupid cops. They were sitting in the lobby as if that would keep him from his wife. He pulled out a key to their condo and slid it into the door. He heard the shower running and felt his erection grow with need. Soon, he promised himself. He walked confidently into the condo. He knew where everything was. It wasn't the first time he'd been there. He smiled at the picture of Allegra with two long pigtails and missing front teeth that hung on the wall. Someday their daughter would be just as cute.

He paused outside her bedroom door and listened to her singing in the shower. He stepped in and frowned. His grip almost broke the box he was holding. The bedding was scattered, and the room smelled like sex. Whore! He closed his eyes and took a deep breath to calm himself. Once he regained control, he silently stepped closer to the bathroom.

Steam and the soft smell of her shampoo reached him as he entered the bathroom. She was right there. So close to him he could reach out and touch her bare breasts, currently being caressed by the warm water. She was so beautiful as she sang with the music coming from the waterproof speakers. Her breasts bounced, her hips shook, and he saw himself there with her. Forever.

Instead of stripping down and joining her, he set the box on the counter and took a step back. Soon she'd do all of this for him whenever he told her to. Soon he'd be the one making the bed sheets fall to the ground in a tangled mess. Soon . . .

After all, it was their destiny.

Chapter Eight

Allegra washed the shampoo from her hair and the cleansing mask from her face. "Finn?" Had she just heard the door again? She wiped the steam from the glass and looked out. No Finn, but a white box sat on the counter. Ah, her surprise! She quickly conditioned her hair and turned off the shower.

Grabbing the large fluffy towel, she patted her hair dry and rubbed the drops of water from her body before picking the box up. She pulled at the white satin ribbon and let it fall to the floor. Allegra bit her lip in excitement as she opened the box and pushed aside the tissue paper.

"Oh my gosh!" Allegra set aside the card and pulled out the sexiest underwear ever. The bra and panties were made of delicate white silk. Allegra shook her head as she relaxed. She had forgotten to ask Finn, but apparently he had been the one who changed out her underwear the other day. He must have a thing for white.

She picked up the note and turned it over. *For Tonight* was typed out on the pretty card. For tonight indeed.

Finn was having a hard time focusing on his meetings. He didn't want to tell Allegra, but every day he grew more and more worried for her safety. With her permission, he had called Damien each of the last two days to see what news there was. Harry Daniels was on the run. He'd withdrawn some money from his account, called in sick at work, and disappeared with his car. But they all knew where he was—New York.

When Finn was with her, he knew Allegra was safe. But he felt anxious when he was in meetings. In the pit of his stomach, he knew this wasn't over. So today he funneled his anger and anxiety into the negotiations.

"Man, I don't know what was in you today, but I like it," Kane said when the last person left the conference room.

"Humph," Finn grunted as he put the papers into his briefcase.

"You got them to almost double their offer. Man, you are the shit!" Kane thumped him on the back and smiled at him.

"I'm glad you're happy, Kane. It's a great opportunity for you. It's also a lot of leverage when your contract with the Golden Eagles comes up next year."

"Damn right it is."

Finn reached into his pocket and pulled out an invitation to the party that was starting soon. "I'll see you and Kelly there. I don't need this anymore," he grinned.

"We'll see you there."

Finn said his goodbyes and hurried out of the building. If he rushed, he could make it back to the condo to change and only be ten minutes late. He couldn't wait to see Allegra. His gut tugged at him just as it did before a big game. He held out his hand and waved down a taxi.

Allegra was used to the routine. Waiting in the hallway as the officer swept her apartment, she tapped her foot impatiently. The day had been a success. The houses she had a stake in were creating major buzz. Celebrities were begging to be dressed by her houses, and magazines were dying to do editorial shoots with them. Overall, Fashion Week had been a big success.

"All clear."

Allegra thanked the officer and hurried to her bedroom. She opened the box Finn sent and pried off her Spanx. They did wonders, but tonight she was going to wear Finn's gift. The soft silk felt cool against her skin. It didn't offer much support, but it looked sexy as hell.

Allegra stepped into the tight silver dress. It hugged her curves and the sides were cut out to expose her upper hips, waist, and part of her midriff. It was a daring dress, but loving Finn made her feel confident enough to take on the challenge.

She reached behind her and struggled to reach the zipper. She circled round and round as she twisted to reach the damn thing. Sweat started to break out, and she was nowhere close enough to zipping it up. She let out a huff and did what any woman would do. She marched out her door, lifted her hair, and turned her back to the security officer escorting her today.

"There you go, ma'am," he said as his fingers fumbled with the clasp.

"Thank you, you're a life saver."

"No problem. I do it for my wife all the time. Are you ready to go now?"

Allegra smiled. "Let's do it!"

"Oh my gosh, your body is to die for."

"Look at those shoulders."

"And the way his waist tapers down into his muscled

thighs."

Finn was flattered, really he was. But he was also cold. "Um, David, Josh, can I put the shirt on now?"

"All right. But only if you promise to model for us once," David told him as he handed him the tailored shirt.

"Isn't that what I'm going to be doing for you tonight?" Finn asked as he buttoned up the shirt. It fit snugly over his body, and the black button-up shirt with silver accent threading highlighted all his best features. With his dark skin, he had a dangerously sexy vibe as well. "Damn, guys. This looks great."

"One modeling shoot," Josh told him again with a smug look.

"Only if it's an editorial about Simpson Entertainment in one of the fashion magazines. And if it is, I get to pose with women I represent. They'll wear both yours and Allegra's clothes while I wear just yours. Think you can make it happen?"

"Please. Did you see how those magazines were drooling at our show? You have yourself a deal, Mr. Williams," David said with a huge smile on his face. "Now, we need to get going, or we'll be beyond fashionably late."

"The horror," Finn said dryly as the group headed for the limo.

Finn sat back and listened to David and Josh talk shop. It was interesting to hear their creative minds at work. Allegra was like that. She could see something completely ordinary or old and, amazingly, turn into something new and beautiful. She could take an idea and make it tangible.

"Here we are. Now, whether you like it or not, we are sending every magazine over to take a picture of you tonight so no leaving early with Allegra, got it?" David teased.

"Got it. And thanks a lot, guys. I didn't want to embarrass Allegra at her big event. I'm man enough to admit I don't know much about fashion."

"Oh, you're man enough all right," Josh said with a sigh as the door opened and cameras flashed.

Finn smiled as he, David, and Josh posed for pictures. He tried not to be that boyfriend who looked all over for his girl, but he didn't need to worry. Some sense inside him told him right where she was. As soon as they had their pictures taken, the men headed to where she was chatting.

"Dammit," Finn whispered. She was talking to both guys he'd encountered in Atlanta and one he hadn't.

"What's the matter?" David asked.

"Nothing."

David and Josh looked at each other and then at the man Allegra was talking to. "The tall one, that's Nate Reece. He's a huge Hollywood action star who we are dying to have as the face of our company."

"I know. He's always all over Allegra. So who are the other two guys?" Finn asked, not taking his eyes off Allegra.

"If it makes you feel better, Allegra said she and Nate have been friends from high school. I didn't get any sexual vibe there. However . . ." Josh started before cringing.

"However, what?" Finn asked.

"However, the man in the $10,000 suit is Asher Woodcroft IV. His family hails from England in the old days of dukes and whatnot. But, they moved to Atlanta at the beginning of the 1900s and are famous for being famous. I really have no idea what Asher does besides sleep with every model, socialite, and actress he can. He has a trust fund with enough money to buy his own country and his goal in life is to enjoy it. I wouldn't trust him. The other guy—I have no idea," David whispered as they drew closer.

Finn had a choice he had to make in a split second. What kind of boyfriend would he be—the overprotective, overbearing type or the man who trusted his girlfriend? It was an easy choice. He smiled as he came up behind Allegra and slid his hand around her waist before dropping a kiss on her cheek.

Finn held out his hand and smiled. "Nate. It's good to see you again. We met at Bellerose." Nate smiled at him suspiciously but took his hand and shook it anyway.

"Yes, it's good to see you again."

"Actually, I'm glad you're here. This is David Bell and Josh Rose of Bellerose," Finn said smoothly. David and Josh shot him an appreciative look before homing in on their prey.

Allegra laughed as the three men headed for one of the small tables in the nightclub. The place was rocking out. Live music erupted from the stage, lights flashed over the dance floor, drinks flowed from the bar, and tables of celebrities from artists to singers filled the club. Kane and Kelly were dancing, and Finn spotted more of his clients from every corner of the entertainment industry.

"Finn, these are friends of mine, Jasper Hale and Asher Woodcroft. And this is my boyfriend, Finn Williams," Allegra introduced.

Finn held out his hand and shook Jasper's hand first. The man only nodded. He was an average-looking man with rectangular black glasses and hipster hair. Finn gave him a small smile before shaking Asher's hand. "It's nice to meet any of Allegra's friends. How are you enjoying the party?"

"It's fantastic. But of course, anything Allegra does is

going to be a hit," Asher said as Jasper looked on at Allegra.

"I couldn't agree with you more," Finn said proudly. Allegra smiled up at him and slid her arm around his waist. He felt like a superhero when she looked at him like that.

"Oh, there's China Kingsley. She's always up for a bit of a good time. If you'll excuse me? Finn, it was nice meeting you," Asher said before heading straight for the actress.

Jasper gave Allegra a serious smile and then turned and disappeared into the crowd.

"I'm so glad you're here. You look so sexy I almost want to ditch my own party," Allegra whispered to him.

"Well, if we can't go home yet, at least we can dance." Finn took her hand and led her out onto the dance floor.

He watched them from the shadows of the party. Allegra should have known better than to think he wouldn't be there. Of course he was there. He couldn't stay away. Even as he pounded back another drink, he tried to calm his excitement. Tonight was the night. Tonight he'd make her his wife. She was trying to deny it, but he'd have her begging for him soon.

He took another drink as he watched Finn holding her tight against him as they danced. If only he could go out there and slam his fist into the guy's face. But he couldn't. Not until his wife was his. So he waited. He waited as Finn ran his hand over the exposed skin along her stomach. He took another drink to keep himself from killing Finn right then. He could get away with it. He was untouchable. But if he did, it would be harder to get Allegra to submit to him.

So he waited. Waited until he saw her leave the dance floor and head to the restroom as Finn went to the bar. His time had come. He pushed away from the shadows and strode confidently to the back of the nightclub. His palms were sweaty with anticipation as he closed in on the door to the women's restroom.

Allegra had never been so hyped before. She had a man who loved her, her line was a success, her houses were the talk of the town, and her after-party was such a hit there was a line around the corner of press and people dying to get inside. She had done it! And dancing with Finn was the icing on the cake.

Allegra closed the door to the stall and hung her purse on the hook. The restroom was quiet compared to the dance floor. And for one moment, she could enjoy being alone. The bass from the music still pulsed in the room, but it wasn't overwhelming. It was a nice reprieve from the craziness outside. She lifted her dress and pulled down her panties.

The door to the restroom opened and the music flooded in, ruining her moment of solitude. She sighed as she stood up and flushed. She was straightening her dress when she paused. It was then she noticed she didn't hear any footsteps. Maybe someone didn't come in? Maybe they changed their minds or accidently opened the wrong door? Either way, it set her nerves on edge. Her mother always told her to be aware of this feeling, and this was just strange.

The sound of Allegra sliding the metal hinge open filled the tiled restroom. She was being silly. She was in a club full of people who knew her. What did she have to worry about? She slowly opened the door and was about to step out of the stall when a shadow crossed the floor. Suddenly the door opened and a rush of models poured into the restroom.

"Oh, Miss Simpson!" Kelly said before introducing her

friends. "Your show was amazing. Thank you so much for letting me keep the outfits I walked in. That was so kind of you."

The models crowded the mirror and fixed their makeup as they all asked Allegra about Fashion Week and told her which shows they walked in.

"Come on, Miss Simpson, we can go out together. Finn grabbed a table with Kane for us. I'll show you where," Kelly said with a bubbly smile.

The girls filed out of the restroom and with one last look back, Allegra could have sworn she saw a pair of men's black shoes under one of the stalls before the door slammed shut.

Chapter Nine

Allegra couldn't shake the feeling someone had been in the restroom with her. It was only a split second, but she knew she saw those shoes. Every nerve in her body told her to run. Instead, she took a deep breath and sat down next to Finn. When he put his arm around her shoulder, she snuggled in closer and stared at the door to the restrooms. She saw some people coming and going, but no one stood out to her. Ever since she'd gotten those flowers, she'd been freaking out at the smallest things. Now she was imagining someone coming into the bathroom.

She was determined to enjoy the night and stop her mind from always going down the dark path. Tonight was a success, and she was in the arms of the man she loved. So Allegra tore her eyes from the restroom and threw her head back to laugh as Kane told her about the Scottish pirate commercial.

Finn held Allegra close to him as people came by the table to talk. He wasn't trying to stop her from talking. He wasn't trying to keep her next to him. Instead, he felt he needed to protect her. Ever since she came back from the restroom, something had been different. She had been pale and a little shaky when she sat down next to him. Then she had burrowed into his side as if she were hiding. Slowly, she'd been relaxing and enjoying herself again, but he still felt her vulnerability.

He leaned down and put his lips near her ear. "We can go whenever you want. I'm yours to command tonight. You just let me know what you want to do."

He enjoyed the fact her face had flooded with color. That got her looking better.

"I'm exhausted. It's two in the morning, and I'm pretty sure this party will go most of the night. Let's make the rounds and then head home."

"Sounds good, sweetheart. I have plans for the night," Finn whispered. He couldn't wait to give her his surprise. He'd taken a massage class and had a bag full of scented candles and massage oil. He couldn't wait to pamper Allegra after her chaotic week.

He followed as she led him around the room saying goodbye to all the people who had helped make this week a success. He smiled, shook hands, and even laughed as David and Josh flattered him.

"We have three reasons to celebrate tonight. First, Fashion Week was a huge success. Two, we landed an editorial for Simpson Entertainment's new VP as he wears Bellerose, and three, Nate Reece has agreed to be the face of our new line!"

Finn smiled as Allegra gushed.

"I didn't doubt for a second you all could land that editorial. I look forward to it. Here's my card. Call me when you're ready for me. And thanks again for tonight," Nate said to David and Josh as he handed them his business card.

"It was our pleasure. Why don't you get the car? We'll walk Allegra out," David told him as he slid Allegra's arm into his.

Finn looked to Allegra, and when she gave a small nod of her head, he kissed her cheek and headed outside.

"He's divine."

"You're keeping him, right?"

Allegra laughed as David and Josh talked over the top of each other.

"Yes, I'm keeping him."

"That's good. I like him, Leggy," Nate said as he strolled over with a model on his arm.

"I'm so glad I have your approval, guys," she said sarcastically.

"Really, he's a good guy. He's smart and down to earth. He is what he is. No pretending, which is rare in this world," Nate told her as they headed outside.

"Thanks. I think so, too." Allegra saw Finn leaning against the limo. They shared a smile, and she knew he knew they were talking about him. What she loved was that he seemed confident and perfectly at ease with who he was. It was something Tigo had been teaching her, but all she really needed was to look at Finn as an example.

She said her goodbyes and got into the limo. It was a short ride back the condo, but she would enjoy every moment. As soon as the door closed, she shifted in her seat to face Finn. The limo was dark with black leather seats and black carpet. A light from the minibar cast a faint yellow glow across the luxurious interior.

"I have something to show you," Allegra said as she kissed him gently. Raising her skirt, she intended to show him she was wearing the panties he got her. The dress was tight and when she tried to shimmy it up her hips, she lost her balance. With a squeak, she fell off the seat and landed with a thud on the floor at Finn's feet.

"Well, that was showing me something all right," Finn said as he tried not to laugh, but his quirking lips gave him away.

"I was trying to show you the panties."

"Trust me, sweetheart, I can see your panties just fine. I just didn't know sprawling on the floor was the best way to show me." Finn bent over and lifted her onto his lap with ease. "Now, let's get a better look."

Allegra's eyes closed as soon as his lips came down onto hers. He cradled her in his lap and kissed her senseless as one hand slowly moved up her calf, then her thigh, and finally to her hip.

She felt a tug and lifted her hips just enough for him to pull the panties over her bottom and drag them slowly down her legs. The soft silk wisped against her skin and sent shivers up her back as his lips worked magic along her neck.

"Hmm. Very nice indeed," Finn said with a smirk on his face as he held up the scrap of fabric that probably cost him a fortune. "Too bad we have to put this on hold. You may want to put your legs down. We're home."

With a sigh, Allegra slid from his lap as he shoved her panties into his pocket a moment before the door opened. The off-duty officer opened the door, looked at Allegra's flushed face and Finn's smug smile, and grinned.

"I'll make a quick tour of your condo and be on my way then."

Allegra blushed harder and Finn's smile just widened. He still held the panties in his hand inside his pocket as they rode the elevator up to the penthouse. He couldn't wait to get her alone inside.

"Wait here, please," the officer said as he made his way

into her condo.

Finn stood behind Allegra and placed a soft kiss on the crook of her neck as they waited. How long did it take to clear the condo? If this officer didn't hurry, he'd come back to find him taking her against the wall.

However, the second the officer came into view with his gun drawn was enough to kill the mood.

Finn tightened his grip on Allegra and felt the moment she saw the officer. She tensed in his arms, and Finn had the overwhelming urge to leap in front of her to protect her from whatever was in her house.

"Ma'am, sir, please come inside and lock the door," the officer said before grabbing his cell phone and calling dispatch.

As soon as he hung up, Finn had to know. "What is it?"

"A message."

"What did it say?" Allegra asked as her voice shook.

"Not so much said as did. Come with me, but don't touch anything. We'll be sweeping the condo for prints." The officer turned and led them down the hallway toward Allegra's bedroom.

Finn held her hand tightly in his, and when they stopped at the door he was afraid she'd faint. The bed was shredded. The feather pillows had large hunting knives sticking out of them and the mattress looked as if someone had tried to rip it apart. White downy feathers covered the room like a fresh blanket of snow.

"It's okay, Allegra. They'll find him," Finn said quietly as he pulled her into his arms. The scene was a message all right, and no words were necessary.

"That bastard!" Allegra pushed away from Finn so fast it surprised him. He knew she would be angry. He just didn't quite expect this.

"I've called Agent Wallace to let him know. But you need to be careful, ma'am. He's escalating."

"Good. The sooner I can get my hands around Harry's throat, the sooner I can kill him!" Allegra cursed some more as Finn and the officer took a step back. They both realized when someone was about to lose her temper. Rumor had it that the rare times Allegra lost it, she *really* lost it.

"Sweetheart," Finn started to say. When Allegra looked at him, he just closed his mouth.

"That little prick thinks he can ruin my life all because I broke up with him. Well, he has another think coming."

"I'm going to call Troy and get the plane ready. I think it's time we go home, Allegra. We can't stay here tonight. Somehow he's able to get in here. It's not safe." Finn took a deep breath and casually slid his hands to cover his balls. "And we need to tell your family." He waited for the kick he thought would be coming, but instead Allegra's shoulders sagged.

"You're right. I have to tell them."

"I'll be right there with you the whole time. Your family loves you."

"I know they do. I was being stupid not to tell them what was going on. It's time to tell them everything. Let's go home, Finn."

He watched them as they climbed the stairs to her private jet. Didn't she see that Finn was just using her for her money? Finn was nothing but a gutter rat and he was endangering his wife. He had to protect her. And he did. He might have lost control a little bit in the bedroom. He was man enough to admit that. But when he saw the panties *he'd* given *his* wife as he stood in the next bathroom stall, and then saw Finn with his arm around her . . . he became enraged. And now Finn was going to feel his wrath. They were going home, and home was where he was at his best.

Margaret Simpson's house was ablaze at five in the morning. Every light in the two-story house in the suburbs was on, and her driveway was filled with cars. Allegra gripped Finn's hand as he pulled his car to a stop in front of the house. The second the car was turned off, a loud rapping at Allegra's window made her jump in her seat.

"Sweet magnolia, Shirley. You scared me to death," Allegra said as she opened the door. She couldn't take any more surprises. Not after the past six months.

Shirley, her father's former secretary who now ran the office . . . rather, spied on the office, stood outside with her walker. No one knew how old she was. Allegra guessed she was closing in on ninety, but it was hard to tell since Shirley acted like she was eighteen. Today's banner on the walker read *Born Sexy*. "Are you knocked up?"

"What?"

"Is there a bun in the oven? Are you in the family way? Did the rabbit die?"

"No!" Allegra cried.

"Then why the heck did you drag us out here in the middle of the night?"

"Shirley," Finn warned in a tight voice.

"Hmmph."

Allegra watched as Shirley turned around and rolled toward the now open front door.

"Are you married?" her mother called out. Margaret Simpson was the epitome of Southern charm. Her red hair was always perfect, and her slacks always had a crease in them.

"What?"

"You know, did you tie the knot? Elope? Did he make an honest woman out of you?" her mother asked as they walked up the sidewalk.

Allegra turned to Finn. "I can't do this. It's too humiliating."

Finn stopped her and waited until she looked up at him. "This isn't your fault. It is his. He's the one with the problem, not you. You should not be ashamed of this, Allegra."

Allegra took a deep breath. "Okay, here we go." She turned to her mother. "No, Mom, we're not married."

"Then why the emergency meeting in the middle of the night?"

"Mrs. Simpson, let's go inside and talk," Finn said firmly.

"Oh no. It's something bad," Margaret's fingers twisted together with anxiety as she hurried them into the house. "I was hoping it was something else. This has to do with why you've been acting differently these past six months, doesn't it?"

"She's been acting differently?" Reid asked from the couch. Her brother was thirty-seven years old, but for some reason he hadn't picked up the ability to read females in all that time . . . even his own sisters, bless his heart.

"Duh," Bree said as she rolled her eyes.

"What is wrong with you, Reid? Even Drake noticed," Elle said.

"Yeah, Logan did, too," Bree told Reid as she held hands with her new husband.

Logan turned to Drake and shook his head. "I don't

know if we've just been insulted or praised."

"I don't either. What's going on, Allegra?" Drake asked.

Allegra gripped Finn's hand and suddenly saw seven pairs of eyes zero in on her. "I've been hiding something."

"Told you she was pregnant," Bree whispered to Elle.

"I'm not pregnant!" Allegra yelled.

Elle's eyes widened and Reid sucked in a breath. "Shit. We've made her mad. Duck and cover," he said in warning to his siblings.

"Okay, enough of this," Shirley said as she moved to sit down. "I was in the middle of a dream about the Thunder from Down Under, and I'm determined to finish it. Now, what is this about?"

"Last year when I broke up with Harry Daniels, he didn't want to take no for an answer," Allegra started.

"I never did like him. He gave me a weird vibe, and you should always listen to your gut," Margaret told the group.

"Yeah, small men usually have small winkies and it makes them irritable," Shirley said as if she were a therapist. "Look at Napoleon . . . small winkie."

Allegra tightened her grip on Finn's hand, but when she looked over she saw Finn struggling not to laugh. Suddenly she felt it. The constriction in her stomach moving up her chest and then it happened—she laughed. For the first time in a year, she laughed about her situation. Finn was right. It wasn't her fault. It was Harry's fault for having a small winkie.

"Well, you were right not to like him," Allegra said as she tried to stop picturing Harry and his small appendage. "He refused to accept that it was over. For six months he tried to win me back by sending me love letters, asking me out, and calling. Finally, I had to tell him there was no chance of us getting back together. I had moved on." Allegra looked at Finn and smiled.

She had fallen in love with him slowly while working together late at night as she helped him with reports. She loved the way he cared so much for her family's company and for how much he respected her sisters and herself. It took a strong man to admit he wanted to learn more, and Finn was unashamed of his desire to learn as much as possible. He was smart and picked up things remarkably fast. It was a major turn-on for her. And then when he took her to his gym, well, she'd already fallen in love with his mind. When she saw him strip off his shirt . . .

"That's when I started getting nasty texts and emails from an anonymous source," Allegra continued.

"Oh, no. Why didn't you tell me, Leggy?" Bree asked. Having gone through something similar, Bree understood the scariness of anonymous threats.

"If I recall, you didn't say anything for a while either," Allegra pointed out.

Bree cringed. She hadn't mentioned anything until a building was blown up with her in it.

"What kind of notes, honey?" Margaret asked, her hands clasped tightly.

"First they asked me out and were signed as a secret admirer. When I said no and told him to leave me alone, they got worse. They called me names. Told me I was his and his alone. That I belonged to him, and then when I got closer to Finn told me I was putting Finn and myself in danger. That he wouldn't tolerate his woman seeing other men."

"Is that what happened at Bree's wedding?" Reid asked.

"Yes. I got over four hundred text messages calling me

a whore."

"I'll kill him," Reid said through clenched teeth.

"Get in line," Finn told him.

Allegra just rolled her eyes. She was so angry, they'd have to beat her to it. "Finally, I confronted Harry after I moved and changed my phone number."

"I thought you said you lost your phone," Margaret said.

"I lost in when I threw it into the ocean." Allegra managed a weak smile.

"But, why did you move?" Elle asked.

"I can't explain it, but I think Harry was in my home. Nothing was out of place, but there were many times when I would wake up and swear I heard something, a creak of a board, the clicking of a door—just *something*. Then there was when I felt as if I had been touched while I slept. I dreamt it, but when I woke up there was the smell of cologne."

Margaret put her hand to her mouth. "Oh my gosh," she whispered. "My baby!"

"It's okay, Mom. I moved. I confronted Harry and threatened to file charges."

"Did he back off?" Bree asked.

"For a while. I haven't gotten any more texts or emails. Everything was fine until New York. I got a delivery of flowers. There was a note from Harry with it. Then when I refused to stop seeing Finn, it escalated. Tonight when we got back from my after-party, my bed was torn to shreds and two knives were impaled in the pillows."

"Why would he destroy your bed?" Margaret wondered.

"Because they've been doing the nasty, playing hide the salami, knocking boots, rolling in the hay." Shirley shook her head at Margaret's confused face. "They were having sexual relations. Geez, after four kids I thought you'd know what those terms meant. What the heck did you call it?"

"We called it getting to know someone biblically," Margaret said a little embarrassed. Somehow, that made Allegra feel better. She'd just been outed as having sex before marriage to her mother, but it was her mother who was embarrassed.

"How scary!" Elle jumped up from the couch and enveloped Allegra in a hug. "I'm so glad you've told us. Is this the reason for your weight loss? I've noticed you haven't been eating as much."

"Or sleeping. You've been looking tired," Bree said as she joined Elle in hugging Allegra.

"It's hard to sleep or eat with all this going on. I never know if I'm being watched or if someone is in my house. I've tried to ignore it. I was in denial for so long, but this is too much. Something has to be done."

"We need to call the police," Margaret said, her face white with worry.

"I've talked with Damien. He notified the local police and state troopers. Further, as soon as I got a threat in New York, he contacted the FBI. All the agencies are working together. Damien has arranged for me to meet with the FBI and local officials in a couple of hours. They've already been looking for Harry. So far, they haven't been able to find him."

"Thank goodness. I won't be able to stop worrying until he's captured. Do you want to stay here?" Margaret asked as she clutched Allegra in her arms.

"I'm fine, Mom. Finn will stay with me. But, I want you all to know what's going on. Maybe we need to restrict visitors to Simpson Global as well for a while."

"Of course," Elle said as she pulled out her phone to email security. "Send me a picture of Harry, and we'll have it in the hands of all security personnel. I'm glad you told us, Allegra. Now we can help you catch this guy."

"You're not worried how this will look? I mean, I'm so weak. I don't want it to reflect badly on Simpson Global."

"Oh, Leggy!" Bree cried as she grabbed her sister's hands. "You're not weak. You are so brave to have gone through this. I'm so proud of you for being strong enough to stand up for yourself."

"You are the victim, Allegra. You did nothing wrong, and you have nothing to be ashamed of. Simpson Global and your family will stand by you and praise you for standing up to this horrid man. By being brave and not being quiet about it, you'll bring light to this issue. Think of all the women and men who suffer at the hands of stalkers because they never report it. Never be afraid to ask for help. Never," Elle said passionately.

Allegra wiped the tears from her eyes. She'd been so embarrassed to admit she was being stalked because deep down she feared it was her fault. But now she wished she'd told them about it when she received the first email. She would make up for it. She would meet with the police tomorrow and find Harry Daniels.

Chapter Ten

Finn sat quietly as he held Allegra's hand. She was showing the investigators all the evidence she had. After leaving her mom's house, Finn, Allegra, and the investigators sat in a twenty-four-hour diner and produced a timeline of all the events. They had explained how tricky it was to prosecute stalkers because victims tended to be in denial for so long that they hadn't collected enough evidence for an arrest.

Allegra had turned over phone records, text messages, and emails. The NYPD sent a copy of their file, and Damien pushed for the investigators to go with a crew to her old house and look for more evidence.

"She said she heard things. I think you should fingerprint the place," Damien told the group.

"It's been over a month," one of the investigators stated nonjudgmentally.

"I still own the house. It's just been sitting empty. No one should have been in it since I left. I hadn't even sent the cleaning crew in. I just wanted to pretend it never existed. Thinking about the house brought back the fears. I had nightmares about someone in my house while I tried to sleep," Allegra explained.

"We can sweep it. It doesn't hurt to try. And this is good," the FBI investigator said, holding up the timeline.

"The question is, how long will it take Harry to make it back to Atlanta? I'll pass along his photo and the information on his car to the state police for all the states between New York and Georgia, the train stations, and the airports."

"If you feel uncomfortable at anytime or get any more messages, contact one of us immediately. You're not alone in this. We'll find him, Miss Simpson," the woman from the police department said as she took Allegra's hand.

Allegra managed a weak smile. She felt better having a team behind her. She now had someone believing her when she said she heard things going bump in the night. For the longest time, she didn't even believe herself.

Finn walked out of the FBI's office with his hand on the curve of Allegra's back. What she must be going through . . . it made him feel both angry and vulnerable at the same time. He had to protect her, but what would he do during the day when he was at work or when he had meetings?

"Allegra, I think we need to call Mallory in on this, too. I'm sure Elle has already filled her in. I don't like the idea of you alone during the day."

"I already did," Allegra smiled as she looked at the leggy blond in black leather pants and red deep V-neck sweater, leaning against the door of an obscenely expensive sports car. "Hi, Mallory. Thanks for coming."

"As if I wouldn't. You're like family to me. So, we're going to be hanging out for a while."

"Until Harry is found, yes."

"I'm having my guys work on that."

"The police and FBI are, too," Finn told her as he pulled Allegra closer to him. He hated the thought of leaving her to go to work, but he'd seen Mallory in action. The pearl necklace at her throat and blond-bombshell, high-society look was just on the outside. Underneath the pearls was a woman who'd kick ass first and ask questions later. Just the type of person he wanted looking out for Allegra.

Mallory smiled. "I'm sure they are. But, my guys don't get caught up in all that legal red tape. They kinda just skip right over it. After all, we're not going for prosecution. We're trying to find him immediately."

"Have you learned anything yet?" Allegra asked as she pushed her hair back from the wind. Winter was coming to Atlanta early this year, and she shivered as another gust hit her.

"He's gone dark. We tracked him to a hotel outside Atlanta, but it was over a week ago. I sent some guys there. They saw security tapes of him with some woman going in for a quickie. The woman left an hour later, and he spent the night. The next morning he drove off, and that's the last anyone has seen him. My guys are tracking the woman down now. After they question her, they'll turn everything over to the investigators. Now, shall we go to work?"

Finn leaned down and gave Allegra a kiss on her lips, a quick kiss that conveyed all the promises he wanted to make to her. "I'm going to be really late tonight. I have a lot to catch up on." When he looked up, Mallory was grinning again. "Take care of her."

"With my life," Mallory promised.

Allegra looked at the pictures the casting director had sent over for the European leg of fashion shows and ground her teeth together. She thought she had made her stance on models clear, but she was looking at everything she told them she didn't want. She tried to stay out of the way of the designers as much as possible, but this was one area she put her foot down. She picked up her phone and waited for the director to pick up. His job was to hire the models to walk for her fashion houses at the various fashion shows.

"Matthew, I'm looking at the pictures of the models you chose," Allegra said without bothering to identify herself or even say hello.

Her mother would be horrified. Mallory just looked up from the corner of the room where she was working on her laptop and raised her eyebrow in question. Allegra held up the pictures, and Mallory frowned.

"You will not hire any of these women. Half of them look like children, and most of them are malnourished."

Matthew sighed over the phone. "Miss Simpson," he said patronizingly, "models can be sixteen years old in Europe when they walk the runway. And this is what is on all the famous runways this year."

"Well, they aren't on mine. Either find models over eighteen and at a healthy weight, or I'll find a director who can. Do you understand me?"

"Miss Simpson, clothes don't fit models as well when they're bigger."

"Bigger? Matthew, I'm a size eight. Am I so fat that I can't wear any of the clothes from my own fashion houses?"

Mallory snorted and Allegra listened to Matthew stutter. "No, Miss Simpson. Not at all. You're lovely."

"Good. Then find more models like me since the clothes look so good on me."

Allegra hung up, and Mallory broke out in laughter. "I almost feel sorry for him. Almost. I don't get this industry at all. Why would I want to buy clothes a child is wearing? She can't go to the clubs I go to. Hell, she can't even drive a car, and she's going to tell me what's sexy? Please."

Allegra closed the binder and sat back in her chair. "I'm ready to go home. This day has been hellish. I'm tired and hungry."

"Let's stop at that place on Peachtree that has those good burgers," Mallory suggested.

"Peachtree Center?"

"No, Peachtree Street."

"Sounds good. Let's go."

He smiled at the cashier as he passed her three hundred dollars in cash. She wrapped up the sexy silk blouse and smiled at him. She would be his type. Young and blond with fake tits and big hair, but he was spoken for now. He could look but not screw.

"Is this for your girlfriend?" she asked him with a hint of suggestion that told him that if he said it was for his sister, she would go down on him in the dressing room.

"No. It's for my wife." He liked the sound of that. The most powerful, sexy woman in the world was his wife. And he'd be the one controlling her.

"She's a lucky woman," she said wistfully.

"I'm the lucky one," he said as he took the bag and headed out the door.

Allegra waited for Mallory to look in all her closets and under all the beds. "All clear," Mallory called. "Looks like you got a present though. Should I worry about it?"

Allegra felt her heart pound and her body shake as she

waited for Mallory to bring the present out of the bedroom. Her mind flashed to the card with the word *Whore* written on it. Instead, it was a white box exactly like the one Finn had given her in New York with her lingerie set in it. She let out her breath and smiled.

"No, that's from Finn."

"I wonder what it is?" Mallory asked as she handed it over.

Allegra opened it and pushed away the white tissue paper. She pulled out the printed message and read out loud. *For you to wear tomorrow and think of me while you do.* She reached into the box and pulled out the white silk blouse.

"Wow! Who knew Finn had such good taste? That's an expensive blouse," Mallory said as Allegra held it up in front of her. The blouse was of such fine silk it was almost see-through. The front buttoned to the top of her breasts and then formed a wide V as it went up to the collar.

"It's beautiful. I'll wear it tomorrow. So, what should we do now?"

"Movie?"

"That sounds wonderful. Put in some popcorn; I'm going to change into my pajamas."

Allegra changed into an old pair of flannel pajamas, tied her long hair into a loose ponytail, and slid on a pair of fluffy socks. She was prepared to relax and even more prepared to get to bed. Knowing Mallory was here would finally let her sleep well and, she hoped, keep the nightmares at bay.

He quietly put the key into the lock and turned the doorknob. It was late and all the lights to Allegra's house were off. He heard the soft click and turned the knob slowly. He stepped into the entranceway and was greeted with a gun barrel to his temple.

"Don't move or I'll shoot you."

"It's me," he said as calmly as possible.

"Finn, do you really think sneaking in was the best idea?" Mallory asked as she holstered her gun.

"I didn't want to wake Allegra. I'll call you when I'm outside next time. Damn, Mallory. I know you're a badass and all, but seeing you in action is something completely different. Would you really have shot me . . . or him?"

Mallory shrugged her shoulders. "I've done it before. But, now that you're here, I'll head out. See you tomorrow."

"Goodnight," Finn said automatically as he watched Mallory pick up her designer purse and slip on a sexy pair of high heels before heading out the door.

Finn locked the door and set the alarm before heading to Allegra's room. He quietly got undressed and slid into bed. Allegra jerked in her sleep. She quickly curled up in his arms as he whispered goodnight. He held her tight as he stared into the darkness over her head. The feelings he had for the woman he held could be overwhelming at times. His desire to keep her safe . . . no, his *need* to protect her . . . came from a primal part of him that was hard to even understand.

How someone wanted to hurt her was beyond him. Allegra was all that was good in the world. She was smart, caring, and sympathetic. She was a natural leader at the same time. She was everything he'd always wished for and never thought he'd have. And somewhere in the pit of his stomach, he wondered if he did have her.

She hadn't met his mother or seen where he was raised. What would she think of him then? Would the differences be too much for her? He saw the looks they got from some of the older generation. That was in the business world where most people tempered their feelings. What would happen when he brought her into his neighborhood? What would old Mr. Browning say when he brought a strawberry blond girl with a luxury car into the neighborhood? Would Allegra turn and run as she realized some of the challenges of being with him? Yet, Terrell hadn't cared. He cared more that Allegra didn't seem to return his feelings. His mother would only care that Allegra loved him. Maybe he did still have a chance. He'd find out sooner or later because at some point in time he was going to have to take Allegra home.

Allegra twirled in front of Finn in her new blouse. She'd paired it with a black pencil skirt for her meetings today. The feel of the shirt sliding smoothly against her skin and caressing her body reminded her of Finn's hands that morning. She should be scared out of her mind with Harry out there, but instead she'd gotten a wonderful night's sleep safe in Finn's arms.

"What to do you think? I just love it!"

"Looks wonderful on you. You look beautiful in everything you wear . . . or don't wear." Finn grinned.

Allegra rolled her eyes. "You're so bad. We have dinner tonight with my family. Are you in?"

"Of course. Your family is practically my family already." Finn slammed his mouth shut. "I meant since I've known your family so long, not because we're married.

Married, who said married?"

Allegra had stopped twirling and stood staring at him. Was he bringing up marriage as if he'd been thinking about it? She hadn't thought about marriage. Had he? She hadn't even thought a relationship was possible, but marriage to Finn filled her heart and made it beat happily in her chest. No, it was too soon. Was there a too soon in her family though? When her sisters had found their husbands, they'd fallen hard and fast.

Allegra stammered, "Well, I have to get to work."

Finn leaned stiffly down and gave her a quick peck on the cheek. "Um, yeah, have a great day. I'll see you at your mom's house?"

"Yep. See you there." Allegra hurried out the door and let out a long breath. That was awkward—way awkward. She pulled out her cell phone and called the one person she could talk to about it. "Oh my gosh, Nate, you won't believe what just happened."

Finn closed the front door when he heard Allegra call Nate. He had gone out to apologize for the uncomfortable exchange they had just had but had frozen when he heard her call Nate. Finn had slunk back inside and quietly closed the door. The worries from last night bombarded him and this one now just added to it. Was she making fun of him to Nate?

Finn felt his heart harden. He knew this was a mistake. He was just too out of her league, and he had to get out while he still had his pride intact. He would wait until the last minute and cancel tonight, claiming he needed to work late. And it would be better to sleep at his place so Mallory didn't accidently shoot him. He felt so betrayed he was sick to his stomach. The empty feeling only worsened as he gathered his things from Allegra's home and left.

He watched her smile and talk animatedly into her phone. She was wearing his present. She was becoming his. He followed close behind her as she made her way to her car in the garage behind her house. He could smell her perfume and inhaled deeply, savoring every scent.

"I can't believe it. I'm so happy. These gifts he's been getting me are so nice and then after this morning, I think he may have marriage on his mind," Allegra said into her phone. She was probably talking to one of her sisters. Power surged through him. He was doing this to her.

"I don't know if he's going to ask. What would I say? I mean, it's only been a short time, but I love him so much. I've known for six months I wanted to be with him. I want to say yes. Heck, I want to yell yes over and over and leap into his arms and never leave them." Allegra laughed as she opened her car door and slid in.

She shut the door, and he could no longer hear her, but he'd heard enough. She was in love with him. He'd known she was going to be his from the first time he saw her, and now he was slowly making her his own. She was wearing the clothes *he* told her to and the lingerie *he* picked out for her. His plan was working. The overwhelming urge to be near her filled him. Soon . . .

Chapter Eleven

Nate stretched out his long legs in Allegra's office and grinned at her. She'd given up working an hour ago when Nate came into town. She'd been gushing about Finn ever since.

"No wonder I couldn't get a hold of you," Elle said as she walked into the office. "Hi, Nate. It's good to see you again."

Nate rose and gave Elle a hug. "It's good to see you, too."

"When did you get into town?"

"Just an hour ago."

"Do you have any plans tonight? We're having dinner at Mom's house. I know she'd like to see you." Elle sat down and kicked off her heels before crossing her legs.

"Is your mom making one of her pies? If so, I'm in," Nate said seriously. Everyone took Margaret's pies seriously because they were so good you thought you'd died and gone to heaven.

"I'll make sure of it when I call to tell her you're coming. So, what's going on? I assume you've told Nate." When Nate nodded, Elle continued. "Has Mallory gotten any leads?"

"She's out trying to work one now. They found the prostitute, but she wasn't any help. It seems there have been a couple of hits on Harry's debit card. He's pulling out large sums of cash. Mallory is looking at the security from the ATMs, but so far there's no luck. Somehow he knows which ATM's cameras are blocked. A teenager stuck his gum on one, and an hour later that's the one he withdraws money from. After he gets his money, it's like Harry seems to disappear off the face of the Earth." Bree sighed as she ended her summary of the investigation.

"Mom's a wreck, as I'm sure you are. She wants to lock you up somewhere until Harry is caught," Elle said.

"Probably in my old room where she can feed me soup, as if it would cure the problem." Allegra loved her mother, but as the baby of the family it had taken her a long time to get out from under everyone's thumb and grow to be her own person.

"Is Finn coming?" Shirley asked as she wheeled into the office. "Hey, good-lookin'. You need a love interest in your next movie?"

Nate laughed when Shirley winked and got up to give her a hug. "It's good to see you, Shirley. I have a feeling you'd turn Hollywood on its ear."

"Ears are not the body part I was thinking of. Anyway, you joining us for dinner tonight?" Shirley asked as Allegra got a good look at the *Ask me about my cure for stress* banner on her walker.

Allegra saw Nate look at it, too. She and Elle shook their heads at him when he was about to ask Shirley about it. "I sure am. Want be my date?" he asked instead.

"You betcha. How do you like your eggs? I want to be prepared for the morning," Shirley winked and Nate burst out laughing.

"No wonder you have to date men half your age, Shir. Otherwise you'd give them a heart attack."

Finn sat in his office and stared at his phone. He was due at Margaret's house in ten minutes. Finally he pulled up Allegra's phone number and sent a text, letting her know he was delayed at the office. He was too confused to see her now. He felt like he was in the middle of a tug-of-war game with his own heart.

When Allegra had explained about Harry, he understood. But how could he understand this? He knew he would have to confront her. He just didn't want to tonight. At the sound of a light knock on his door, he looked up.

"Miss Eddie, what can I do for you tonight?"

"I think you know perfectly well what you can do for me tonight," Raven purred as she dropped the trench coat she was wearing.

Allegra looked down at the text from Finn and frowned. He told her he was wrapped up at work and would see her tomorrow. She missed him so much already and maybe it was silly, but she wanted him with her family. Suddenly the fun festive dinner was no longer that. She felt alone at the table as her family and friends teased each other.

First Mallory ditched her and sent some rent-a-goon in a very expensive suit. Not that Shirley minded. Shirley was currently trying to tell him how sex relieves stress and is good cardio. But when Finn ditched her, she wondered if she'd done something wrong.

Damn Harry. He was ruining friendships and relationships. It took her months just to trust Finn enough to tell him what was going on, and now she had the feeling that she got the brush-off tonight. She would have to talk to him tomorrow. Maybe Harry threatened him. Finn loved her; she knew he did. Threatening her was the only reason that Finn would back away from her. This relationship meant too much for her to sit back and do nothing as it fell apart.

"Here, honey, have a piece of pie. It'll put a smile on that beautiful face," her mother said as a slice of pumpkin pie was placed in front of her.

"Thank you, Mom," Allegra smiled. She felt better. She wasn't going to sit back and watch life happen to her. No, she was going to take a page out of her sisters' book and go after what she wanted.

"You know what else will put a smile on your face . . .?"

"Shirley!" the women all groaned as Nate and Reid laughed. The bodyguard could only cringe.

He slid the key to his house into the lock and turned the knob. The alarm beeped and he smiled to himself as he entered Allegra's birthday. The alarm continued to beep, and his smile slid from his face. He entered his soon-to-be mother-in-law's birthday, but the alarm continued to beep. He pushed back his anger and concentrated. He knew everything about her, and he knew he'd get the right passcode. He thought about Allegra and what she held the most dear. Then he smiled and entered the day she first started Simpson Fashion. The alarm turned off, and he straightened up.

He ran his gloved hand along the granite island in the kitchen and opened the cabinets. It felt like home. His wife had found them the perfect place to live. He opened the refrigerator and took the last beer. He twisted off the cap and took a long drink as he walked into the living room. He took a seat on the couch and picked up the remote. Turning on the television, he was able to catch the last few minutes of the basketball game as he finished his beer.

The game ended, and he grabbed the bottle by its neck and stood back up. He meandered around the living room. There, over the gas fireplace . . . that's where he would put their wedding picture. He'd have it done in oils and it would be the centerpiece of the room. He thumbed through her DVDs and smiled when he saw his in there. He'd been bringing more and more of his things over during the last couple of months. He was glad they hadn't been damaged in the move.

He pulled out one of his movies and put it on the television. Tonight, when Allegra turned it on, she would think of him. He walked through the formal dining room where he pictured Thanksgiving dinners and then into the master bedroom at the back of the house.

He set the beer down on the side table and lay down on his bed. Breathing deep, he smelled Allegra on her pillow. The slight mixing of her soft perfume with her own essence was enough to make him close his eyes, dreaming of them together in their bed.

Finally he dragged himself from the bed and wandered into her closet. He touched her clothes and picked out his favorites. She needed more white clothes. She looked so beautiful, so innocent, in that color. He pulled out a drawer and found her nightgowns. Most of the time she wore T-shirts or flannel PJs, and they were cute. But if he was going to be coming home after a long day of work, he wanted her to look her best. Now he knew what her next gift would be.

He opened another drawer and found her panties. He

saw the white ones he had gotten her and smiled. Glancing around, he saw the white blouse as well. Yes, he was slowing making her his.

Walking out of her closet, he headed into her bathroom. He opened the medicine cabinet and looked around. Anti-inflammatory, gel shoe insoles, birth control . . . He grabbed the contraceptive pills and made sure she was taking them. Sure, he wanted her to be pregnant with his child, but not until he'd had his fill of her. Then she could quit her stupid little hobby to stay at home raising their children and hosting parties for him. He knew the first time he saw her that was her destiny. Looking around the house only confirmed what he already knew—Allegra Simpson belonged to him.

Finn hit the bag over and over again. Sweat trickled down his face, his arms, and his bare chest. He didn't bother to wipe it away. He just continued to vent his frustrations on the bag. Hit after hit allowed his mind to go blank.

Finally his arms shook with exhaustion, and he stopped. Breathing deeply, he took off the boxing gloves and tossed them on the bench. He picked up a towel and wiped the sweat from his eyes. When he looked up, Tigo was standing there with his arms crossed and a glare on his face. "What?" Finn asked.

Tigo just raised one eyebrow. The man was in his late fifties and was as close to a father figure as Finn had. His dark black hair was parted on the side and had a streak of gray in it. "You have to ask?" he said in his slightly Hispanic-accented voice.

Finn shook his head and wiped the towel over his face

again. "You don't know what's going on."

"I don't? You bring a young lady and her family here. They're nice," Tigo continued. "You'd have no idea they were rich. They seem to care about everyone here, from the janitors to me. You personally train with Miss Allegra, and I see the way you look at her—eyes full of love. Then you stop coming together. Yet she comes to see me and has Tigo train her. She asks me to teach her to defend herself . . ."

"It's not that. I would never hurt her," Finn defended.

Tigo placed his hands on his hips and narrowed his eyes at him. "I think you've already hurt her. Not physically. No, you would never do that. But let Tigo finish. She wants to know how to protect herself from a man trying to sneak up on her. She wants to learn how to be aware of her surroundings and how not to freeze up if she's scared. She wants to find her own voice, her own power. What does that tell you?"

"She's being stalked. It's an ex-boyfriend who wouldn't take no for an answer. I know all about him."

"Ah, so she trusts you enough to tell you when she wouldn't even tell Tigo. Then ask yourself this, would a woman scared out of her mind not want the man she trusts with her?"

"I thought she did, but every time I turn around she's running to another guy. A movie star," Finn said with an eye roll. "Let's just face it. I'm some kid from the hood, and she's so above me. I was naïve to think it would work."

"How long have I trained you?"

"Since I was a stupid kid," Finn said with a soft smile.

"Bah! You're still a stupid kid. You know how to fight. You have confidence and cunning, yet you're telling me a peacock can win your woman?"

"Do you know Shirley?"

"No, who is this Shirley? Why would I know her?" Tigo asked with a wave of his hand.

"I'm pretty sure you're her long-lost son." Finn laughed. Tigo looked confused and Finn laughed even harder. "It's a compliment. She's very wise."

"Ah, then I look forward to meeting her. Now, get your head out of your *culo* and do what a real man would do to win back the woman he loves."

"Fight for her?"

"Ha, no . . . beg." Tigo laughed as he turned around and headed for his small office.

Finn laughed as Tigo's shoulders shook. Finn had never been a quitter, yet fear was holding him back with Allegra. He was going to confront her and Nate to find out what was going on. It couldn't be worse than not knowing the whole story. And if Nate was looking for a fight, then Finn was going to give it to him. He loved Allegra heart and soul. One way or another, tomorrow she was going to know it.

Chapter Twelve

Allegra hurried through her emails. She was meeting David, Josh, and Nate for a photo shoot in fifteen minutes. Last night had been miserable. She hadn't slept at all. Every time she took a deep breath, she caught a tease of a scent in the air that wasn't hers or Finn's. It scared her even though she knew the alarm had been set, and she was probably imagining things.

There was no sign of Harry Daniels. He had disappeared, so the idea that he was just walking around Atlanta was crazy. But somehow she couldn't shake the feeling that she was being watched. Yet, when she turned around, no one was. Add that Finn still hadn't called her, and it made for one sleepless night.

Her phone rang, and she picked it up without taking her eyes from her computer. "Allegra Simpson," she answered distractedly.

"Hi, Allegra. It's Jasper."

"Hello Jasper," Allegra mumbled as she typed out an email.

"I didn't get much of a chance to talk to you in New York, but I'll be in town for a Golden Eagles game this weekend. I didn't know if you wanted to join me."

"Oh, thank you for the invite, Jasper. But I'm afraid I'm so worn out I hope to do nothing but sleep this weekend.

Finn might be there though."

"Then I'll keep my eye out for him. Again, it was a real pleasure seeing you. I hope we can do it sometime soon."

Allegra stared at the phone after she hung it up. She was surprised. That was the most she'd ever heard Jasper say for as long as she'd known him. She wondered why he was calling now. Maybe Asher was right; maybe Jasper did have a thing for her.

"Hmm, so it's true," Shirley said as she wheeled into the office.

"What is?"

"That you and Finn are screwing up the best thing y'all have ever had."

"I don't know what you're talking about."

"Really, because you both look like crap."

"Then he shouldn't have ditched me last night. I didn't do anything." Allegra slumped back in her chair. "Well, I didn't, but Harry has. Who in their right mind would want to date me with some crazy guy out there?"

"I don't think that's it. By the way, who's Tigo?" Shirley asked with interest.

"He's the owner of the gym we go to. Why?"

"I heard Finn muttering about if I was younger I'd be perfect for Tigo."

"You heard him muttering?"

"Okay, I heard him talking to Kane, and I might have been down the hall with my ear pressed to the wall. When I turn these puppies up, I get great reception," Shirley admitted as she tapped her hearing aids. "Hmmph, if I was younger . . . I'd show him."

Allegra managed to laugh as Shirley rolled out of the office. The security guard with Mallory's firm stepped inside with a familiar box in his hand. "This came for you. It looks clean."

Allegra jumped from her chair and raced to grab it. Finn hadn't forgotten about her. She tore it open and pulled out the typewritten card. *I'm sorry I missed you last night. This is for you to wear and think of me at night.*

She unfolded the tissue paper and pulled out a slinky white silk nightgown, if it could even be called that. It was beautiful. Finn really wasn't mad at her. He really did have to work. She shouldn't have let her emotions run wild with her like that.

"I have the car out front. I'm ready whenever you are," the guard said with a slight blush to the top of his ears as he averted his gaze from the sexy sleepwear.

"Perfect. Let's go." Allegra grabbed the box and her bag and hurried to the car. Her mood lifted; she was about to spend the day with her friends and the night with the man of her dreams.

Allegra walked side by side with her bodyguard. The photo shoot was only a few blocks away so she decided to walk it. It was a nice fall day. The leaves were turning vibrant colors and the bite to the air was invigorating, especially after a night with little sleep.

"Allegra!" a man's voice called out from behind. Her bodyguard whipped around and stood in front of her.

"It's okay; it's a friend. Hi, Asher," Allegra called out from behind a wall of man.

Asher laughed as he came forward with an older man and woman Allegra instantly recognized from the papers and magazines as his parents. "Fabulous accessory. By Milan, everyone will have one," he joked.

Allegra laughed, too. She did feel a bit ridiculous, especially here in Atlanta. At the same time, she couldn't forget the feeling that she was being watched. Even now. "He's very handy."

"Mother, Father, this is Allegra Simpson. She runs Simpson Fashions, part of Simpson Global. Allegra, this is my mother, Georgiana Woodcroft, and my father, Asher Woodcroft III."

Allegra shook their hands and pasted on her fake society smile to match theirs. "A pleasure," she purred.

"The pleasure's ours. How do you know Ash?" his father asked.

"Allegra is a friend of mine, Father. We run in all the same circles," Asher replied for her.

Allegra laughed. "Not all. I'm mostly here in Atlanta. But, yes, we've heard about each other for so long through all of our mutual friends. And then we finally got to meet at the beginning of this year. We've been friends ever since."

"I saw her show in New York, and it was a huge hit."

"Really?" his mother asked. "What kind of clothes do you make?"

"Clothing for the professional woman. Something that can make her feel good about herself at the workplace without being too exposing or too boxy."

"Intriguing. I'll have to look at them. Would you care to join us for lunch? We are just heading to a little place down the street."

Allegra smiled kindly. Sure, they were a little stiff, but it seemed they had good hearts. "I'm so sorry, but I have a fashion shoot with Nate Reece."

"Nate?" Asher III asked. "That name sounds familiar."

"Yes, he was in New York with me. We're very close. He's an actor, but he's doing a commercial shoot for one of my houses."

Recognition dawned. "Ah, yes. A playboy just like my

son."

Allegra's smile froze in place, but Asher laughed. "I don't know if I can even compete with Nate." Asher shot her a wink and chuckled again. "He's a nice guy. I partied with him at his club, NITE."

"Yes, he is." Allegra smiled at the group. "It was nice to meet you both."

"Likewise," Mrs. Woodcroft said with a soft smile.

Allegra gave one last smile and a wave. She turned to follow her new fashion accessory, but she'd only made it a couple steps before her phone buzzed. She dug it out of her coat pocket and stopped in her tracks. *Whore.*

"He's here," Allegra gasped. She whirled around, her gaze darting to every shadow and window. All she saw were people walking. The Woodcrofts were walking away from her, people from Simpson Global were coming in and out of the big glass doors, but no sign of anyone watching her.

"Come on, Miss. Simpson. Let's get you to the photo shoot and then call the investigation team. I'd rather get you out of the open as quick as possible."

He put his arm around her and tucked her against him. He was like a boulder protecting a pebble, and it made her feel better as they hurried down the street. The phone beeped again, and she looked at the screen.

Too many men, not enough time, huh, Allegra?

"He's watching me. Oh God, why can't they catch him?"

"I don't know, but I've got you now." He pulled out his phone and pressed a single number. "Code Red."

Rushing away so soon? We have so much to talk about. You're mine, Allegra. Don't forget it.

Allegra had never been happier to get off the streets

before. She hurried into the studio, and her bodyguard shut the door and locked it. Everyone from the photographer to Nate stared at her.

"What's going on?" Nate asked worriedly.

Allegra's hands shook. "He's here. He saw me talking to Asher. He flipped out and starting texting me."

"Have you called the investigators?"

"Yes, I notified our office and everyone is being contacted now. They'll be here shortly," her bodyguard told them.

"What's going on?" David asked as he and Josh came forward.

Allegra felt like an idiot for getting so worked up over some text messages, but she was freaked out. "I'm being stalked by an old boyfriend who doesn't want to let me go. He followed me to Fashion Week, and now he's back here."

"Oh, honey. That's horrible. Guys!" David called out to get everyone's attention. "I want this place locked down tight. I want someone at every door. I don't care if that means we do makeup in the stairwell, you got it?"

People started moving as they grumbled to one another about crazy designers. Allegra gripped his hand. "Thank you for not telling them why. I'm just so embarrassed for all the trouble this is causing everyone around me."

"Nonsense. You have to be careful. We all understand that. My sister's ex-husband stalked her. He's in jail now, thank goodness. It was scary," David told her.

"Yes, and my friend Rusty was stalked as well by some woman he bumped into at the grocery store. Thank goodness she went away after the police talked to her. The important thing is to be safe. And you have this beast of a man—I totally mean that in a good way," Josh said to her bodyguard. "It appears you're taking all the right steps."

"Thank you so much, guys. Enough about me," Allegra waved her hands and looked over the set. "Before all the cops get here, let's get some photos done."

Finn shut the door as soon as Kane left and dialed Allegra's extension. He talked to her secretary and found out she was at a photo shoot. Should he wait for her to get back or should he go to the address Allegra's secretary had given him? He stared at the address and thought of going another minute without talking to Allegra. The answer was easy. He shoved his chair back and sprang to his feet. In two long strides, he was across the room with his coat in hand.

He hurried down the hall and tried to dodge all his employees wanting a moment, which he knew would turn into thirty minutes. He buttoned his coat as he hit the sidewalk and strode quickly toward the location of the photo shoot.

What was he going to say? Did she even realize he had blown her off last night? Was it too much to show up at her photo shoot? No, he loved her, and he was tired of all these misunderstandings. The only way to know for sure was to talk to her. He wasn't going to just assume the worst and blow his best chance at love.

He found the location and went to open the door, but it wouldn't budge. He knocked, and the door was flung open by a huge monster of a man. His beefy hand shot out and grabbed Finn by the coat. Finn broke the hold and jumped back.

"What the hell?"

"Mr. Williams!" The man sounded surprised. "I'm so sorry, there was an incident and . . ."

"Incident?" Finn pushed through the door. "Is Allegra . . .?" What he was going to ask died as he looked at a half-naked Nate Reece with his arms wrapped around Allegra, laughing. She kissed him on the cheek and then playfully swatted at him when he smacked her butt.

"I'll give you an incident," Finn muttered as he reached Nate in no time. He pulled Allegra out of Nate's arms and slammed his fist into Nate's pretty face before Allegra even had time to scream.

"Oh my gosh! Finn, what are you doing?" she yelled as she went to her knees beside a bleeding Nate who was sprawled out on the floor.

"Lawdy," Josh whispered somewhere behind him.

"I think the better question is what are *you* doing? I come here to talk to you and you're all over a half-naked man?"

"It's not what it looks like," Allegra stuttered as she turned red. She looked quickly between Finn and Nate. "I swear."

"Hard to swear when I just saw it, Allegra. I've waited and waited for you. I've trusted you with my heart and then this? It's over. God, I've been so stupid." Finn spun and was out the door at the same time the first investigator pulled up to the curb.

"Damn, that hurt," Nate moaned.

"Oh, Nate. Are you okay?" Allegra asked as she tried to stop the tears from falling down her cheeks.

"I'm fine. You need to go after him."

"And say what? He's not going to believe there's nothing between us. It was hard enough the first time when he saw us outside my building." Allegra sighed and sat back on her heels.

"I'm sorry, Leggy. I know we play around, but it never occurred to me how it would look." Nate lifted his head as the makeup artist rushed to his side.

"It's okay, Nate," Allegra looked back at where the investigator stood. "I have to go talk with them. The photos so far are fantastic."

Allegra tried to smile as she walked over to the investigator. She was pretty sure he was the one from the FBI. He looked like a young gun who would someday run for office. He had perfectly cut sable hair, a suit that was a little nicer than should be worn in the field, and a killer smile.

"Looks like I'm changing my number again." Allegra just handed it over to him after unlocking the screen to show him the messages.

"Thanks. We'll get to work on these text messages. With your permission, we'd like to hold your phone and keep this line open. We want to see if he sends you any more messages."

"Oh," Allegra looked at the phone questioningly. What if Finn tried to call her? And she had all her work stuff on the phone. Maybe Drake could help. "Let me call my brother-in-law first, if you don't mind."

The investigator handed the phone back to Allegra. She scrolled through her numbers and called Drake.

"I'll be right over." And he would. His office building was less than two blocks away.

"Please tell me you've figured out something," Allegra begged when she hung up the phone.

"We have. We've been digging deeper into Harry Daniels. It appears this isn't the first time he's stalked a woman. He's had to move four times in the last five years because of police investigations. I talked to the sheriff in Knoxville, Tennessee. As soon as the police are brought in, Harry disappears. He moves out of state where it's hard to track him down. So far there have been reports filed in Arkansas, Alabama, Mississippi, and Tennessee."

"Are there warrants out for him?" Allegra asked hopefully. Then he could stay in jail in every state and not get out for a long while.

"No. There was never enough evidence tying him to stalking. Just like in your case. We need to compare his handwriting to the note on the flowers, get a security tape of him buying them, or fingerprints from him breaking into your condo—something—or we can't arrest him."

Allegra wrapped her arms around herself and held tight as she tried to keep from shaking. "You're telling me if you don't find that evidence, then you won't be able to arrest him when you find him?"

The investigator looked gravely at her and nodded. "That's right. We need something more. Something we can hold in our hands and show a judge. Unfortunately, you haven't provided that. You haven't seen him to make an identification. And you waited so long to report it, we don't know what kind of evidence has already been lost."

Allegra started shaking, and then she felt angry but wasn't sure if her shaking was out of fear or anger. "Me? I need to get the evidence? Then what good are you?" she yelled.

The makeup artists froze. David and Josh took a step back and everyone held their breath.

"Excuse me?" the investigator asked slowly.

"What? Do you want me to repeat that? If I have to gather the evidence, what's the point of having you involved? Because you sure as hell haven't done anything else to help me. You're not stopping him from texting me, from following me to New York, from breaking into my house . . . How are you going to stop him if he decides to take a knife to me instead of my bed? Would that be enough evidence for you? Oh, no, because then I'd be dead and *I* wouldn't be able to identify him!" Allegra's hands had dropped to her side, clutched in tight fists.

The photo shoot seemed to be frozen in place. No one moved. No one breathed as they all stared at the interaction between Allegra and the investigator. He didn't seem to realize the danger he was in because he shot Allegra a condescending look as he held up his hands. "Look, you need to take a breath and calm down."

The entire room sucked in a collective breath as they cringed. Allegra turned five shades of red. "You don't tell me to calm down when you can't do your damn job and find him," she said in such a cold voice David and Josh took another step back.

The door opened as Elle and Drake walked in. Elle took one look around and immediately wrapped Allegra in a protective hug. "What happened, Leggy?"

Allegra tried to answer but she had started shaking again, and this time it was definitely in anger.

Nate cleared his throat. "Mr. FBI Dumbass over there decided to blame Allegra for not gathering evidence to arrest Harry even though he's been investigated for stalking in four other states."

Allegra felt Elle stiffen next to her. She pivoted slowly on her sexy designer heels. "You did what?" she asked the investigator.

"I just told her the truth. If she can't handle it . . ." He shrugged.

Drake just shook his head. "It's sad. You don't even know what's coming, do you?"

"I don't think you understand stalker cases. They are very hard to prove, especially if the victim . . ."

"That's right, the victim," Elle cut in. "And you just criticized her. It's time for you to leave."

"Sorry, this is my case and I'm not leaving."

"Yes, you are," came a soft Southern voice. Mallory leaned against the door with her perfect wavy blond hair and natural makeup. "I've already called the director."

"The director?" He laughed. "Just who do you think you are? The Director of the FBI doesn't take calls from civilians."

Mallory smiled, and Allegra shivered for a whole new reason. Mallory's smile looked deadly—like a long silver rapier cutting you to shreds without you even realizing it. "My name is Mallory Westin, and he takes my calls."

The investigator's phone rang, and when he looked at it, his face paled. "Hello, sir."

He nodded a couple of times and then listened for a minute. "Yes, sir." He hung up the phone and looked at Allegra. "I'm sorry I was insensitive to your feelings. I'm sorry for my behavior. Ms. Hectoria will be here shortly to look over your phone and discuss the case further."

Allegra watched him turn and walk out the door. Once it closed, the whole room breathed again. "Oh, now I feel bad. I didn't want to get him fired or anything."

"Don't feel bad," Mallory said as she came to stand with her and Elle. "He's had several complaints lodged against him. His daddy's in politics, and he wants to be, too. The complaints haven't gone very far up the ladder. It just so happens my daddy's a bigger player than his."

"I'm sorry you had to play your father card," Allegra said quietly. She knew Mallory hated to depend on her father, one of the highest-ranking senators in Congress, for anything.

"Don't be sorry, Allegra. Really. I would use it in a

heartbeat to protect one of you all. You're my sisters." Mallory wrapped her arms around Elle and Allegra and squeezed. "Now, what happened?"

Allegra explained and then handed the phone to Drake. He looked at the texts. "He did have a point about leaving the phone on. But, I think it would be better if you were the one answering the texts. Have you ever thought about doing that?"

"I did at first, but then he just kept asking me out over and over again. I stopped answering and then the texts turned mean, and I didn't want to respond. I'd just change my number, but he always seems to find me."

"Stalkers are pretty smart. Smarter than most criminals in fact," Mallory chimed in.

"It appears so," Drake said as he held up a little chip between his fingers.

"Damn," Mallory muttered.

"What's that?" Allegra and Elle asked at the same time.

"It's a tracker. He's known exactly where you are at all times."

Allegra felt the room spinning. "How?"

"I don't know. He could have picked it up anytime you set your phone down. He could have broken into your house and put it in. He could have picked your pocket and then put it back. Either way, it means he's been near you."

"I knew someone was following me." Allegra couldn't describe it but she felt so violated. How had he gotten so close to her?

"I'm going to clone this phone. What should I do with the tracker?" Drake asked Mallory.

"I know. Get an old phone that matches hers. We know he's watching. Allegra, when you leave here, I need you to make a very public display about dropping your phone and breaking it. Then give it to Drake. Drake can slip the tracker on it and tell you he'll dump it in the garbage at his place and get you a new phone. That way he can have the tracker, and it won't make Harry suspicious. But, he'll try again to put another one on it, so we'll have to be careful and hope we can catch him this time."

Allegra's phone beeped in Drake's hand and seconds later Elle's did, too. Drake cringed and covered the phone so Allegra couldn't see.

"What is it?"

Elle sighed. "You've gone viral."

Chapter Thirteen

Finn ripped off his suit jacket and hung it in his locker at Tigo's. He had to meet with Raven Eddie in an hour, but if he didn't work out his anger on the bag, he wouldn't be able to control himself around her.

He slid out of his pants and pulled up a pair of athletic shorts. Walking barefoot into the gym, he slid on his boxing gloves. "Anyone up for a fight?"

"Sure. Let's do it, old man," Hugo, Tigo's newest boxing champ, said as he slid under the ropes.

Finn just smiled as he slid his mouth guard in.

Tigo leaned against the ropes as he watched Finn pulverize his newest protégé. Hugo was good, great in fact. But he couldn't stand up to Finn's extra weight and intelligence. Finn was a smart fighter. Hugo hadn't learned that yet. Finn landed a solid uppercut to the chin, and Hugo went down.

"Okay, don't kill my next prize fighter," Tigo interrupted as he lifted the rope and walked onto the mat to slap Hugo's face. Hugo's eyes fluttered as he came back around. "Next time don't call him old."

Hugo moaned and rolled over onto his stomach and threw up. Finn smiled. That had felt good.

"So, you're in a fighting mood today? Fighting here, fighting there, fighting everywhere," Tigo said as he handed Hugo off to another coach.

"What are you talking about?" Finn asked as he spit out his mouth guard and held out his hands for Tigo to help him take his gloves off.

Tigo reached into his pocket and pulled out his phone. He handed it to Finn as he worked on his second glove.

"Holy shit."

"That picture of you punching Hollywood's sexiest man has gone viral. Apparently someone got the shot with their cell phone and it's everywhere."

Finn looked at the image of his fist connecting with Nate's mouth and felt his whole world break away. Allegra would never forgive him. In one stupid moment of anger, he'd ruined everything. Of course, Allegra had already done that by cheating on him, but now the reality that it was definitely over hit him hard.

"When I said you could fight for your woman, I didn't really mean to beat the competition up," Tigo laughed. "Now, if it was the man terrorizing Allegra, that's different. But, Hollywood Hottie, not what I was talking about."

Finn rushed to get ready as all the guys teased him about punching Nate Reece over Allegra. It was everywhere. The radio, TV, and social media were all blowing it up. One of the online magazines was reporting she was pregnant with Nate's baby, and that's why Finn lost it.

He walked into his office, trying to shove it from his mind. Last time Raven came into his office, she'd dropped her coat to reveal nothing but a teddy. Finn had kicked her out of the office and planned to never talk to her again until she broke out the tears and the pleading. He agreed to one more meeting, but only if she proved herself to be a serious businesswoman. Finn wasn't hopeful. However, he didn't know why, but one of the cable stations actually thought a reality series with Raven had potential, and he was going to present it to her shortly.

"Well, now that you're single, I think we have a lot more to talk about than just my new television show," Raven purred as she slinked into the room.

Finn steeled himself for battle as she took a seat on the edge of his desk.

He couldn't stop looking at the news. Allegra was everywhere. She had made a fool of him. She was supposed to be *his* wife, and she was caught in a love triangle. How would that make him look?

He clenched his fist and slammed it onto his desk. The wood splintered, and his hand throbbed as more and more commentary came from the dumb entertainment news correspondent. She'd embarrassed him, and now she'd learn her lesson. He opened the drawer and pulled out a knife. Oh, yes, she would learn she belonged to him and only him.

He opened his laptop and pulled up the tracker. She was still at the photo shoot. He'd see her soon . . .

Allegra walked out the door with Elle, Drake, Mallory, and Nate. The photos were amazing, and Bellerose was going to have one heck of a spring campaign. Allegra had her arms full of sample clothes and laughed when Mallory told her to laugh. Somewhere in the shadows he was watching. She felt it. He couldn't know how upset she was, or he might catch on to the plan to draw him out.

"Let's do something tonight to celebrate," Nate said, following the script Mallory had given them.

"Sure, let me just check my calendar." Allegra reached for her phone and as soon as she got it in her hand she stumbled. The clothes started to fall and she dropped the phone to the ground. As she tried to regain her balance, she dug a heel into the screen.

Drake reached out to steady her and Elle grabbed the clothes. "Damn," Allegra cursed.

Mallory picked up her phone and grimaced. "Sorry, Allegra, but I think you broke your phone."

"No. It has to turn on . . ." She fumbled with it for a second. "Nothing."

"Let me see it," Drake said, holding out his hand. He fiddled with it for a second and then shrugged. "It's trashed. I have some phones in my office though. We can toss this one, and I'll give you a new one."

"Really? Thank you." Allegra smiled at her brother-in-law as he slid the broken phone into his pocket.

"You go with Drake. I'm going to get back to work." Elle gave her hug. "Great job. If he's watching, he'll totally buy it," she whispered.

"Thanks. You married a good one," Allegra said a little wistfully as an image of Finn came to mind.

"I'll come with you. I want to see what kind of toys Drake has in his inner sanctum," Mallory teased as she moved closer to Allegra.

"I better be on my way. Thanks for today. I'll see you tonight to celebrate." Nate kissed her cheek and walked off with Elle as Allegra went into Drake's building.

As soon as the doors to the elevator closed, Allegra let out a long breath. "Do you think he bought it?"

"If he was outside, he did. Who knew you were so good at acting?" Mallory asked as she tried to lighten the mood.

"On one hand, I hope he tries something. On the other, I'm scared to death he will," Allegra told them as she wrapped her arms around herself once again.

Mallory dug into her purse and pulled out a stun gun. She turned it on and gave it a test zap. Electricity sizzled in the air. "Then you have this. Keep it within reach at all times—even at night. Now Drake, show me all the really cool stuff."

He followed close behind. He wasn't going to lose his chance. A lesson was needed and that was exactly what Allegra was going to get. He turned down a block that housed the fashionable *who's who* of Atlanta. He walked on the opposite side of the sidewalk and had to duck behind a car a time or two. He had to be careful. He didn't want to give himself away too soon.

The door to the townhouse closed, and he moved closer. He crossed the street and slid into the narrow driveway on one side of the home. He could see lights being turned on and a shadow passing in front of one of the windows above him. He tried to see, but the windows were too high off the ground.

Looking around, he decided to head for the small backyard. He followed the driveway and stuck to the shadows. It was still light out, and he didn't want a nosy neighbor to spot him. The backyard housed a small garage with decorative evergreens on either side of the garage door. He looked back at the large French doors and waited until the coast was clear.

He darted across the pavement and slid behind one of the trees, pressing himself against the wall of the garage. He was shielded. No one could see him. He was so smart. He'd never get caught. He smiled as he pushed his hand through the tree and made a hole to watch through.

For two hours he didn't move. He watched everything—picking out what clothes to wear for tonight, turning on the television, texting on the phone, undressing to take a shower . . . people really needed to learn to use their shades. Lucky for him, they always thought they were safe inside their home.

His time came as the door to the bathroom closed. His breathing was slow and steady as he unfolded into the darkness. He pulled up the hoodie and tied the strings so it wouldn't fall down. He tugged his leather gloves up and walked around the tree. He strode across the small manicured lawn and up to the French doors. He slid his knife between them and with a flick of his wrist he heard the latch click.

He opened the door and quietly stepped into the house. He made his way to the bathroom in seconds. He slid his black-gloved fingers through the small crack of the door. Slowly he pushed the door open. The water turned off, and he stepped back quickly. Short shower, must be running late.

He pressed himself against the wall and waited. He heard her drying her hair and slapping her feet on the marble floor. The door opened wide and steam rushed into the bedroom.

His hand tightened on the knife, and he held his breath. A foot came into view and he made his move. Spinning around, he grabbed for the shoulder with his free hand as the knife slid into the freshly washed skin.

Screaming. He loved it when they screamed. But then a fist came at him. He had been enjoying the screaming too much and had lost focus. The fist slammed into the side of his head. The room tilted and the bathroom door slammed shut. He looked around quickly and saw the cell phone was gone. Then he heard talking on the other side of the door. Dammit! He'd blown it. He scrambled to his feet, shook his head, and then darted out the back door.

He pulled himself over the brick privacy fence and hurried through a couple of yards with no lights on. When he came out onto the street, he pulled the hoodie down and slowed his pace. He heard sirens in the distance. They wouldn't find him. He was safely away in less than thirty seconds. He continued to walk to the small restaurant district and took a seat at the window of a bistro. He smiled at the cute waitress and ordered dinner. Maybe he'd fuck her tonight. Allegra deserved it after all.

Chapter Fourteen

Allegra's lungs burned and there was a pain in her side. She reached for the curtain and yanked it open. Nate lay on the emergency room bed with a white bandage around his midsection.

"Oh my God, Nate!"

Mallory stepped next to Allegra and looked over at the new FBI investigator sitting next to Nate's bed. She stood up and held out a card. Her short, dark brown hair was slicked back with a clip and her face was free of makeup. She didn't need it. She was lovely.

"Agent Hectoria. I'm sorry to meet you this way, Miss Simpson," she said as Allegra took her card. "Mr. Reece was stabbed during a home invasion. He had the presence of mind to tell the EMTs to contact me. He thinks it was our guy."

Allegra's hand covered her mouth as she gasped. "Please tell me you're all right."

Nate gave her a weak smile. "I'm fine. I got a punch in and was able to surprise him enough to dive back into the bathroom. Luckily the knife didn't hit anything. The doctors said I'll be really sore, but I'll be good to go for my movie shoot. Plus, look at all this free publicity I'm getting."

"Don't joke about this. First Finn and now Harry. This is the worst day of my life," Allegra said sadly.

"Speaking of Mr. Williams," Agent Hectoria cut in. "Are you sure it wasn't him? He has already exhibited signs of aggression toward you today."

"I'm sure. What I did see of this man's face told me he was Caucasian. And, to be fair, Finn did have a reason to punch me today."

Allegra blushed as the agent looked at them both. "So, you two are together?"

"No," they both said.

"We've been best friends since freshman year of high school," Nate told her. "We're about as close as you can get without being a couple. Trouble is, people never seem to believe us."

"Well, it could be Harry saw the picture from this afternoon and jumped to the conclusion everyone else did. This is speculation, but my guess is he saw it and snapped. He probably wanted to take his competition out."

Allegra gasped. This was her fault. "What about Finn?"

"I'll send someone over to check on him," Agent Hectoria said as she sent a text. "Are you and Finn together?"

"Maybe? Finn broke up with me, thinking the same thing every news outlet is saying." Allegra's shoulders slumped. It was dangerous to be with her. She either broke your heart or set you up to be stabbed by a stalker.

"Allegra, don't do this to yourself," Mallory whispered. "You are the victim here. You did not cause any of this."

"Miss Westin is right. You're not to blame, Miss Simpson," Agent Hectoria told her as she shut her small notebook. "I'm leaving a police officer with you, Mr. Reece."

"I'm sure Patty has already hired a security team," Nate said with a roll of his eyes.

"And who is Patty?" Agent Hectoria asked quickly.

"My personal assistant," Nate tried not to roll his eyes. His assistant was the queen of organizing, but she tended to go overboard. He was sure he'd have ten hulking men surrounding him from now on.

Agent Hectoria just nodded and then left the room after telling them to make sure they called her if they thought of anything she needed to know. Allegra sat in Agent Hectoria's vacated chair and placed Nate's hand in hers.

"I'm so sorry, Nate. This is all my fault."

"Leggy, knock it off. Don't let this bastard win by getting in your head. Come on, this makes me a real-life action star. The news media and movie studios have been calling nonstop. So, don't feel bad, please."

"Only you could turn this into a positive. But, you're right. This is Harry's fault, not mine. I will feel better if you leave town after you get cleared by a doctor."

"No way. You're my best friend. I'm not leaving you."

"Then as my best friend, you'll leave for me. Take advantage of the press, get lots of movie deals, whatever. But please get out of Atlanta for a while. I'll be able to focus on catching this guy then."

Nate let out a long breath. "I don't like it, but fine. I'll leave tomorrow. But you," Nate looked at Mallory, "take care of her for me."

"I will." Mallory looked like she couldn't wait to get her hands on Harry. Unfortunately, everyone was hitting a dead end. Her investigation had found no evidence of him since the night he rented a hotel room with cash and then withdrew some money a little while later.

"Get some rest, Leggy. They'll get him. This story has gone national. Everyone will know about Harry soon. Someone will see him, and then he'll get caught."

"I hope so, Nate." Allegra had become so accustomed to living in fear she didn't know what she'd do once he was found. She'd be free. Did she even remember what that was like?

"Finn Williams," the woman standing before him stated rather than asked, "I'm Agent Hectoria. Did you stab Nate Reece tonight?"

Finn felt the blood drain from his face. "What? Nate was stabbed? Is he okay? Is Allegra safe?"

Agent Hectoria gave a stern nod of her head and relaxed her shoulders. "Can I come in?"

Finn opened the door wider. "Of course."

Finn listened to the FBI agent fill him in on what happened and then confirmed he had been in a meeting with Raven Eddie when the stabbing happened.

"Take this as a friendly warning. You seem to care a lot about Miss Simpson, but I would stay away from her for a while—at least in person. Harry has now proven he's not above resorting to violence if he sees you as a threat."

"Thank you." Finn showed the agent to the door and then made sure all the doors and windows were locked. It wasn't like Allegra would be leaving Nate's side for a while. He'd had his chance to win her back and had lost his temper. He was just lucky Nate wasn't pressing charges. Elle had already called and ripped him a new one for putting the company in the middle of this drama. Mary, the head of PR for Simpson Global and also a cousin to the Simpson sisters, had called and they'd developed a plan on how to spin the story to minimize damage to Simpson Global. So far it was working. Nate was the bigger name, and he was getting the lion's share of the media attention.

His phone rang, and he had to smile as he saw Shirley's name. "Hi, Shirley."

"Hey, stud muffin. You really screwed the pooch today, huh?"

"You think?" Finn asked dryly.

"Nate got it right; he was mostly naked. Now if you had been naked and there was jello involved . . ."

Finn couldn't help it; he laughed.

He opened his eyes to the morning sun. Dammit, he'd done it again. He slid naked from the waitress's bed. Guilt washed over him like it always did after a night of sex. He should be saving himself for Allegra. But when he got frustrated, nothing fixed it better than a good fuck. He should know better. It was never worth it in the morning.

He looked over at the naked woman in her bed. Her bare breasts raised and lowered as she breathed. Red marks circled her wrists and ankles where he'd tied her up. He liked it that way. The control he had . . . the control he was going to have over Allegra. He ran his hand through his hair. He needed to apologize.

Allegra jumped at the knock on her door. She was dressed for work, but still waiting for her coffee to finish brewing. She and Mallory hadn't slept much the previous night. Mallory held up her hand to indicate she would answer it, then picked up her gun and walked to the door. The knock came again as she leaned forward and moved the window curtain to the side.

Allegra saw Mallory's shoulders relax as she turned off the alarm and opened the door. "It looks like Finn sent an apology gift," Mallory said as she took the box from the deliveryman.

"He shouldn't do that. It was my fault." Allegra took the small white box and opened the card first. "I'm sorry for yesterday. I love you," Allegra read out loud.

"Well, that's a good start, right?" Mallory asked.

Allegra didn't answer her as she lifted the lid of the square box. Inside sat a beautiful strand of white pearls. She ran her fingers over the smooth orbs as her mind raced. Did he forgive her? Did he want to get back together?

"Nice. I'm telling you—who knew Finn had such good taste?" Mallory asked with appreciation. Her own hand went to the strand of pearls that had belonged to her grandmother. As far as Allegra knew, Mallory never took them off.

"They're lovely. I need to get to work and see if Finn's there," Allegra grinned as she took the necklace out of the box and fastened it around her neck.

Finn groaned as someone banged on his door. He cracked his eyes and looked at the clock. Damn, he was late for work. The banging continued, and Finn groaned. "I'm coming!" he shouted.

He shoved down the sheets and picked up a pair of athletic shorts from the floor. He hopped into them as he made his way to the front door. The pounding continued as his cursing increased. Finn reached for the door and yanked it open.

"What the hell . . . Nate?" Finn started through his blurry eyes.

"Morning, sunshine."

"I had nothing to do with your stabbing," Finn groaned as he opened the door. He couldn't handle Allegra's boyfriend this early in the morning, or ever.

"I know you didn't. Wheel me right over there, will ya?" Nate was already giving orders in Finn's house. Letting out a long-suffering sigh, Finn opened the door and took hold of the wheelchair.

"I'm sorry; I'm tired, and there's a lot going on. What are you doing here?"

"My assistant is on her way with an army of bodyguards, but I wanted to talk to you before she got here."

"Why?"

"Because you're the best agent around. At least that's what I hear."

"Oh thanks, Nate. I appreciate you buttering me up while stealing the woman I love from under me," Finn shot at him. The cocky bastard just grinned larger. "You find that funny?"

"I do, and I'll tell you why in a couple minutes. Wait until you meet my assistant, Patty. You two are going to run my life."

"I don't want to have anything to do with your life," Finn spat.

"Too bad. I want you to be my agent."

Finn felt his eyes widen in surprise. "What? Aren't you with another agency?"

"Nope. I heard it on a good authority I should come over to the new Simpson Agency."

"I'm not taking you on as a client. You're not going to try to buy my forgiveness. You're not good enough for Allegra. You know that, don't you? Here you are leaving when she needs you the most. I know it's hard for you, but I can't imagine how scared she is right now."

Nate's smile slid. "Sign me as a client with a confidentiality clause, and I'll tell you exactly why you're right."

Finn ground his teeth as he thought. Nate was Hollywood's new shining star. He'd be stupid not to sign him. "Fine. But I won't be your agent."

"If you feel the same way after I tell you why I'm not a match for Allegra, then I can live with that," Nate said seriously.

Finn tried to calm down, but his muscles were bunched with tension. Was it some kind of game for him to see how many women he could sleep with? Without saying a word, Finn walked back to his office and snatched a copy of the Simpson Entertainment contracts from the printer.

"Here," he shoved it at Nate. Finn tossed him a pen and waited as he read through the contract.

Finn tried not to rip it from Nate's hand and punch him again. He wasn't naturally prone to this much anger, but if Nate was dumping Allegra and running away like a scared boy, then Finn was afraid he was going to lose it.

Finn took the signed contract and set it on the nearby living room table. Nate took a deep breath and looked up at Finn.

"What I say here is not to be repeated to anyone—including the agent you assign to me, should you choose to do so." Nate was so serious Finn stopped being mad. What was going on?

"Only Allegra knows this. And she knows exactly why she and I would never work," Nate told him.

"Okay," Finn said slowly.

"I'm gay."

Finn blinked. He looked at Nate and laughed. He laughed so hard he thought he might cry. "That's the best damn news I have ever heard." Finn shook Nate's hand happily.

"That wasn't the reaction I was expecting when I told the first person about my sexuality," Nate said slightly shocked.

"Are you kidding? This is great news. It means Allegra's not in love with you," Finn smiled. Relief poured through him. "So, when Allegra told me it wasn't what it looked like . . ."

Nate laughed. "Exactly. She was stuck between telling you the truth about me and losing you. I shouldn't have put her in that position. That's why I'm here."

"Thank you. You didn't have to do this."

"Actually I did have to do this. I have a plan we want to discuss with you after you win the girl back and beat the crap out of Harry. Deal?"

"Deal," Finn said as he enthusiastically shook Nate's hand. "Where you are going?"

"I have a cabin up in the mountains in North Carolina. Here's my phone number and my email." Nate handed Finn a piece of paper with the information.

"I'll get to work on some deals for you while you're recuperating. Your old agent will still be in charge of the projects he's already brought to you. Bring any new ones to me."

"Will do. I actually fired my agent three weeks ago. Allegra had told me all about you. I knew I was going to sign with you, providing you treated Allegra as she deserves. And you do. All this time I was taking advantage and mucking it up for you by hiding the truth of who I am. I'm sorry for that. I have a stack of movie scripts to go through for you to negotiate. That is, if you want to be my agent."

"You bet I do. Now, if you would excuse me, I have a woman to win back."

Chapter Fifteen

Finn said goodbye to Nate and and ran for the shower. In record time he was running through the lobby of Simpson Global. "Hold the elevator," he shouted. A walker stuck out and the doors opened again.

Real Men Know Women Only Get Better With Age & I'm Near Perfection. Finn read the large banner on Shirley's walker and imagined what he and Allegra would be like when they were older. He liked it. Holding grandchildren in their arms as their children talked to them. That was perfection.

"Big day for you, huh?" Shirley asked as she pushed the button to Allegra's floor.

"Yes. I'm going to win her back, and I'm not going to let go this time."

"Finally figured out Nate was gay, huh? Bet you feel silly thinking she was cheating on you with him."

Finn whipped his head over and down to look at Shirley's upturned face. "You knew?"

"Of course I did. It was so obvious. He overplayed it when I hit on him. Dead giveaway."

The door opened, and Finn just watched as Shirley turned up her hearing aids and started to wander down the hall. He was sure she was getting the morning scoop on the happenings at Simpson Fashion before heading up to Bree's floor and seeing what was going on at Simpson Construction.

He stepped out of the elevator and walked down the long hall to the corner office. He could see Allegra sitting at her desk staring out the window overlooking downtown Atlanta. Finn was starting to realize the quieter the person, the more layers they had. He never would have thought sweet, innocent Allegra would be strong enough to still be standing after all Harry had done to her. She was strong in a silent, resistant way that blew him away.

Finn passed her secretary and made his way into the office. She turned around and looked at him with yearning in her eyes. Finn smiled at her and stepped to the large bank of windows looking out at the employees. He turned the rod and closed the blinds.

"We need to talk," he said softly. "Nate came to see me this morning."

Allegra's eyes widened in surprise. "He did? What did he want?"

"I'm so sorry for behaving like a jackass. I should've trusted you."

Allegra jumped up from her desk and hurried over to him. "He told you?" Finn nodded and Allegra threw her arms around his neck. "It's my fault. I should have told you more. I love you, Finn."

Finn opened his arms and Allegra fell into them. He ran his hand over her silken hair and held her tightly to him. "I love you, too. We have to stop doing this and start talking about what's going on in our lives."

"I agree," Allegra leaned back and put her hand to a beautiful pearl necklace. "Does it look good? I really love it."

"Yes. Everything looks good on you," Finn lowered his

voice as he nipped at her bottom lip. "From now on, no secrets."

"No secrets," Allegra agreed as she tilted her head back and offered up her lips.

Shirley smiled and started whistling a jaunty tune as she passed by the office. She was happy to take the good news to Elle and Bree. Then she heard the knock on the office door and the secretary telling Finn he had a call from Miss Eddie. The curse words that came out of little Allegra Simpson had Shirley smiling wider. She finally picked up on some of what Shirley had been teaching her.

"Tell her I'm busy. And call Kirk and tell him he has a new client. I'm handing Raven off to him. Then wish him good luck."

Shirley heard the door lock and something on the desk fall to the ground. Oh boy, oh boy! Things were getting interesting around here.

He used his key to open the door and then turned off the alarm. He sauntered into Allegra's house with all the familiarity of living there. Guilt washed over him for sleeping with that waitress, but Allegra had forgiven him. She always did whenever he slipped. She saw him for him and still loved him. Would he stop sleeping around? No, but Allegra would remain his. She was perfect like that. He saw his gift around her throat this morning. It was so sensual he almost came forward to claim her right then and there. It had taken all his restraint not to do so.

He had a plan, and he was going to stick with it. But now with these tempting outside influences gone, she would give all her attention to him. Just two more gifts to give her, and then he could set the finale of his plan into action.

He went to her utility closet and pulled out the stepstool. He carried it down the hall to her master closet. He opened it and climbed up the stairs to the attic entrance. He pushed the wood door up and slid it over so he had enough room to pull himself up. The attic was at an angle, and he had to bend over to make his way to his destination. He stopped at the air ducts and set down his bag. He pulled out a screwdriver and carefully pried a section loose. Looking through the vent, he saw her bedroom.

Pulling out the tiny camera, no bigger than his fingernail, he attached it to the ductwork. He had retrieved the cameras from her old house a couple weeks ago. It was time to see what Allegra was up to so he could prepare for the grand event. He turned it on and then sat back on his heels while he booted up his laptop. He ignored the few live images of their old house, now sitting empty, and pulled up the new camera. He'd kept three small cameras there just in case she went back. A clear image of her bedroom came into view with her bed right in the middle. Good.

He put everything back in place and crawled a little farther into the attic. He stopped at the bathroom vent and repeated the process. When he turned on his laptop, an image of the vanity and glass shower came into view. He moved quickly as he put cameras in the living room and kitchen.

He slid from the attic and used a portable vacuum to clean up any dust that had fallen onto the hardwood. He walked around the house once again. It felt so right to be so near her. The sound of a car door shutting sent him to the window. It was Allegra. His heart beat faster and his palms started to sweat with the anticipation of touching her.

This time he wasn't going to leave. He'd already locked the door and rearmed the alarm when he arrived. Instead of leaving, he headed for the coat closet near the living room. He closed the door just as the front door opened.

"I'll just be outside, ma'am," a deep voice said. Good girl. Being safe again.

"Thank you." Allegra's sweet voice washed over him. Even with a door dividing them, it felt as if she caressed him.

He grabbed the doorknob and slowly turned it. He waited and listened to her set down her keys and her purse. She always put them by the door. Silly girl, she tended to forget her purse if she didn't. When he heard her turn into the kitchen, he opened the door slightly. He could see her back then. She was reaching for a bottle of water and humming. She leaned forward and put on the digital music player. He'd programmed it just for her. Their song played, and she moved her hips to the music as she took a drink of water.

Allegra reached forward again and pressed a button. Music poured out of hidden speakers throughout the house. His girl stopped in front of him and did a shoulder shimmy as she bent to pick up her coat. He moved to the back of the closet and watched as she opened the door all the way. She reached inside and took a hanger from the rod. She did a little spin and then put her coat in the closet before closing the door.

He pulled out his laptop then and turned on the screen. He watched as she made her way to her bedroom and pulled her shirt from her pants. Her fingers made quick work of the buttons, and he couldn't wait for them to be on his body. He opened the door then and walked toward her bedroom. He closed the laptop and looked into the open door. She was bent over pushing the pants from her legs. She wore the panties and bra he had given her. He stepped forward. He was so close. He reached his hand out to her but then she moved. She walked into the bathroom before he could touch her.

Allegra reached into the shower and then whipped around. She could have sworn she heard a creak in the floorboards over the music she had put on. But no one was there.

"Hello?" she called out. She grabbed her towel and wrapped it around her body before stepping back into her room. It was empty. She walked through her house, but didn't see anyone or anything out of place.

She dropped the towel and slid out of the panties and bra Finn had bought for her. She stepped into the hot shower and moved to the music as she washed her hair. Out of her peripheral vision, she saw a shadow and jerked around.

"I thought you could use some help."

She laughed. "Right on time, Mr. Williams. I need help washing my back."

Finn shot her a grin that made her insides melt as he stepped into her shower.

What was that bastard doing here? He sat in his car on the street behind Allegra's house and watched on the laptop as Finn stepped into the shower. What a whore she was. He buys her things, and she sleeps with other men. Well, he'd handled Nate, and he would handle Finn, too. But first his wife needed a reminder of whose clothes she wore and whose jewelry was around her neck as someone else screwed her.

He pulled out his cell phone and started typing. She would remember him, and she would stop this adultery. And if she didn't . . . well, he'd gotten rid of one of her men already. He'd just get rid of another.

Finn woke to pounding on the door. "Sweetheart, is Nate back?" he asked as he pulled Allegra closer to him. She wiggled against him as they spooned and at that moment he didn't care if the President herself was at the door. She could wait.

He cupped Allegra's bare breast in his hand as he nuzzled her neck. He pulled her hips tight against him as he ground against her. His lips kissed their way down her neck and over her shoulder.

The banging continued, and finally Allegra let out a frustrated breath and got out of bed. She slid on a sweatshirt and yoga pants. Finn watched her storm from the room, and he felt very sorry for whoever was disturbing their morning. He lay back in bed and rested his head on his hands as he waited.

The scream Allegra let out had him jumping from the bed and running naked for the front door. He slid to a stop when he saw Margaret, Elle, Drake, Bree, Logan, and Reid standing at the door holding vases of white roses.

Finn lunged for the kitchen and grabbed the first thing he could. He covered himself with a washcloth and stood there trying to act casual.

"Um, Finn dear, I think you need something a little bigger than a washcloth. It's still peeking out at us,"

Margaret said as she averted her eyes and found a sudden interest in the floor.

A white head poked through the wall of Simpsons and let out a whistle. "He's a keeper all right," Shirley told Allegra as Finn prepared to die of embarrassment. Allegra hurried to the closet and pulled out a blanket. He wrapped it around his waist and tried to keep calm.

"Finn, look," Allegra said in a shaky voice as she pointed to the flowers. Now that the embarrassment faded he remembered Allegra's scream of fear. A feeling of dread filled him. He remembered the last time she'd gotten flowers like that.

"Where did those come from?" he asked as Allegra's family filed into the apartment and set down the flowers on the table.

Margaret straightened. "They were delivered to me at the hospital. It seems Harry's done his research. He knows I volunteer at the Children's Hospital in the morning."

"Ours were delivered to our house," Elle told them.

"Same with ours," Bree added.

"Not me. Mine found me at the hotel with a date," Reid said, sounding pretty pissed off.

"You don't have dates at eight in the morning," Shirley pointed out. "You have walks of shame at eight in the morning."

"Ewww," the girls all groaned.

"But the point is he knew where I was," Reid explained.

"You're always at the hotel. It's finished and the grand opening is in a few months. Of course you're going to be there." Bree rolled her eyes like she was about to say *duh*.

"Either way, I also have my apartment here. So the fact he knew to send it to the hotel and not to my apartment means he's not only watching Allegra, but he's watching all of us. Elle, you and Drake live off the grid. But he found you."

Finn put his arm around Allegra and felt a tremor run through her. Reid was right; this just became a lot more dangerous.

Allegra reached over and plucked all the cards from the flowers. She opened the first card and pulled it out. *Your daughter is a whore.* She opened the second. *Your sister is a whore.* She didn't need to open the others.

"Well, now we know why she didn't answer the phone," Shirley teased as she wiggled her bushy eyebrows at Finn.

Suddenly the scary notes were forgotten as all eyes turned to her and Finn. Her mother raised one eyebrow at them. Allegra felt as if she were eight years old again and in trouble for sneaking a cookie before dinner.

Oh no. She was going to crack. No one could withstand her mother's silent stare. She wanted to blurt out she was having the best sex of her life with Finn, and that's why she didn't answer the phone. No, that didn't explain the depths of it. She was making love to the man she wanted to marry . . . marry? Wait. They hadn't gone there. Well, he did kind of bring it up that one morning. They'd only been together a month. But, they had spent the time beforehand getting to know each other and becoming good friends. She certainly had feelings for him the whole time. Was she sure about wanting to marry him? No. Yes. No. Yes.

Finn cleared his throat and drew her from her internal debate. "Mrs. Simpson, I love your daughter very much. I'm sorry we were . . . occupied and didn't hear the phone. It won't happen again. Allegra's safety is the most important thing to me."

Yes. The answer was definitely yes. She'd gone and fallen madly in love with Finn Williams.

The next hour went by in a blink of an eye. The flowers were turned over to Agent Hectoria, as her family all dealt with the uncomfortable situation of finding Allegra and Finn naked together. Finally the flowers and notes were taken away, Finn was dressed, and her family was clustered around her door ready to leave.

"We'll see you tonight for dinner, won't we?" Margaret asked in a way that suggested she really wasn't asking.

"I'd love that," Finn said calmly.

How did he do that? Her stomach was hosting a NASCAR race inside her.

"Wonderful. It seems we have some good news to talk about instead of all this . . . unpleasantness." That was her mom, always looking on the bright side.

Allegra kissed her mom, gave Shirley a hug, and exchanged meaningful glances with her sisters as she saw her family out. She closed the door, turned, and saw Finn smiling at her. He stepped forward, put his large hands on her hips, and smiled down at her. His forehead came to rest on hers and so slowly, he skimmed his lips against hers.

"I love you, Allegra. I love your family. I will do everything I can to keep you safe. We promised last night—no more secrets. But there's another thing I want to promise you. I promise to love you, cherish you, and stand beside you. You're the best person I know, the real you."

"The real me?"

Finn chuckled. "You're already the best person I know. I know you, and I know there's so much more inside you've kept hidden under all your *P*s and *Q*s. Every now and then, it escapes when you're really mad. But that passion simmering down there—that's the real Allegra Simpson."

Allegra gulped. No one, not even Nate, knew that side of her. "So you want me to be mad?"

"No," Finn smiled. "I want you to be you. If you get mad, then get mad. That passion can manifest itself as happiness as well. Let go, Allegra, and just be yourself."

"But, what if you don't like that me?"

Finn moved his hands up her sides to cup her face. "I already love her. And when you find her, tell her there's something I've been waiting to ask her."

Allegra's breathing was ragged to say the least. Did she dare break free of the quiet politeness of her life and spread her wings? What if she fell?

"Don't worry, I'll catch you," Finn whispered right before he captured her lips more firmly. She felt all his hardness when he pulled her tight against him. Her arms clutched at his shoulders as they started stripping their clothes. Allegra let her mind go blank. She stopped thinking. She stopped being nice. She just felt . . . and oh gosh, did she feel—over and over again.

Chapter Sixteen

Finn lay panting on the living room floor. Allegra was slumped on top of him with a satisfied look on her face. Just like he thought she'd be when she let loose. He was proud she trusted him enough to show him this side of her.

Allegra had only shown him glimpses of her true self over the past six months, and his soul cheered in recognition of its mate. He'd known from the beginning he wanted to marry her. He'd known it during the long hours they worked together—and the times they laughed at each other at the gym. He'd known it when he was still just a driver going to night school, and he knew it now as he held her to him.

"I love you," he said, his voice rough with emotion.

She snuggled into his chest, and he felt her lips move to a smile. "I love you, too. Thank you."

"For what?"

"For being there to catch me."

"Anytime, babe. Anytime."

He sat in his car and tried not to throw his laptop through the windshield. She was *his*. He'd claimed her even before this nobody came into her life. He had handpicked her out of all the others to be his wife. It was fate, yet she kept challenging it.

Allegra would wear his gifts, then act the whore for other men. Well, no more. Once she was his he'd keep her far away from other men. She would only serve him. He opened the small box of pearl earrings and slipped in the note for her. He'd have to woo her back. If all went well, by next week he'd have her on her knees begging.

For my own perfect pearl. May our love only grow until the day we say I do. Allegra set the note down and opened the box. Two large pearls sat in the cushion of the jewelry box. Oh my. She ran her fingers over them and laughed. She hadn't known this kind of happiness was possible after her string of bad boyfriends.

Finn was thinking about marriage! He wasn't afraid to talk about it. Was she? No, she wasn't. She knew when she woke from her orgasmic coma this morning that she and Finn were connected on a deeper level. A level she'd seen between her sisters and their husbands. And now she had it.

Allegra twirled around in her office chair as she put on the earrings. Finn wanted to marry her!

Finn shook hands with the agent for Sports X. They had energy drinks, deodorant, clothing . . . everything. And they wanted Kane to add to their X Team. Damn, today had been a good day. It was easy to forget the flowers after the amazing sex followed by two deals that would bring his agency to the top of the game. But more important, he had Allegra.

Oh shit, he had to pick Allegra up for dinner. He was

going to be in so much trouble if he arrived late to the family dinner after being caught red-handed . . . well, not so much his hand, with Allegra this morning. He had seen the looks Reid, Drake, and Logan gave him. Dinner was going to be a slow and torturous affair.

Finn stood staring at three intimidating faces. Reid was swirling a glass of bourbon slowly in his hand. Drake took a sip of his drink and pursed his lips. Logan rocked back on his heels and grinned.

"This is so much fun. Now I understand why you all did this to me," Logan whispered conspiratorially to Reid and Drake.

Finn downed his drink and looked into the flames of the small fire pit in Mrs. Simpson's backyard. Moments ago, the women had separated them by a maneuvering tactic he still couldn't pinpoint. But, here he was, outside with the guys.

"So, Finn. I trusted you with my sisters and this is what I get?" Reid said as Logan snickered.

Drake elbowed him in the stomach and Logan coughed. "Yeah. Trusted you."

Reid and Finn ignored him. "Then you knew they were in good hands. I would do anything for those ladies."

"Not anything, you better not," Drake said dryly before taking another sip of his bourbon. Drake was more of a techie, but you wouldn't know it when you looked at him. He was almost the same height as Finn, and with dark hair and an angled face, he looked rather menacing. More dangerous than Reid, but that was probably because Finn knew all about Reid's jet-setting ways and the fact that he didn't take life too seriously.

"I would never do that, and you know it," Finn said angrily. These guys were his friends. They should know it, and Finn was insulted by the mere suggestion of it.

"What happens when things get difficult between you and my sister? I've seen you both run scared before."

"You have a point, Reid," Finn said. "When that happened before we didn't talk. We were more concerned about what others thought than how we felt. Sometimes you have to suck it up and just put your feelings on the table. We've done that now, and we'll continue to do it. There will be no more running. Don't tell Allegra, but I already know I want to marry her. Allegra needs to decide how she feels before I ask her. She needs to discover who she is."

"She already knows who she is," Reid countered.

Finn just shook his head. "Then maybe you don't know your sister like you think you do. She's doing it already though. She took time to work it out, and now she's finding the confidence to actually try it. And I'm supporting her with this. When she finds her own voice, you'll find a whole new Allegra Simpson. That's when I'll ask her to marry me. She needs to know I'll love every aspect of her, even if she's not the nice girl all the time or if she voices her own opinion, laughs too loudly, or dyes her hair purple. She needs to find that expressive side and know I'll love her all the more for it."

Logan and Drake nodded. "Cheers to that. Welcome to the group," Drake told him as he lifted his glass.

Allegra choked on her drink. Literally choked on it. She was sputtering and coughing right along with her sisters.

"What?" Shirley asked innocently. "He should do porn

with a ding-dong like that. I've heard there's good money it in. Maybe I should try it."

Her mother sat next to them with her mouth open and stared at Shirley with shock. "Shirley! We don't need to be discussing my future son-in-law's . . . *winky*." Margaret dropped her voice and leaned forward so that they could hardly hear her say it. But then she sat back up suddenly.

"He is going to be my future son-in-law, right?"

Allegra rolled her eyes. "That's none of your business, Mom. I shouldn't even think about it until Harry is caught, and I can actually focus on my future."

Margaret held up her hands. "Sorry, it's just that I really like him and would love for him to become part of our family."

"I know, but this isn't your call. It's mine, and I won't be pressured into it."

Bree clapped. "Bravo, sis! And for the record, we're not pressuring you. Well, at least Elle and I aren't. We like Finn—love him, in fact. You'll know if you want to marry him, and only you need to make that decision."

"Very true," Shirley added. "And you may need to sample the goods a couple more times to make sure he's really the one."

Bree snorted and Allegra laughed. She would definitely be taking Shirley's advice. What she didn't tell them was her heart already knew the answer. She and Finn were already a couple. A couple who had learned to respect, trust, and express themselves. She wasn't afraid of messing up anymore. If she did, Finn loved her enough to pick her up and dust her off. That knowledge was actually freeing. She wasn't afraid to say the wrong thing, to make mistakes. In fact, it was empowering.

Allegra laughed with her family, and for the first time,

shared exactly what she thought and shared some crazy ideas for the company. It felt wonderful to express her opinions, and she felt a surge of energy as Elle listened and told her they were good ideas.

"Who is this new Leggy?" Bree asked with a sly smile. "I wonder who, I mean what, has gotten into her?"

"Bree Ward!" Margaret swatted her daughter.

"What?" Bree asked as she copied Shirley's look of mock innocence. "I like this side of her."

"Me too," Elle said as she smiled at her.

"Thank you." Allegra reached out and clasped her sisters' hands. They all looked at each other and Allegra read the support in their eyes. She'd never be afraid to fail again.

Mallory's butt was frozen. She was pretty sure she'd lost feeling in it an hour ago. Atlanta was in the south, and she wasn't used to cold weather. It may be fifty degrees outside, and some might think that wasn't cold, but she'd been sitting on the cold damp grass for too long and couldn't feel a thing.

She held the binoculars to her face and stared at the man she despised. Reid was laughing with Finn, Logan, and Drake outside of Margaret's house. Flames were casting a warm glow on his face. His square jaw had a hint of stubble on it, his straight nose with a hint of a crook . . . he looked heavenly, and all she wished was to damn him for being happy when she couldn't be.

From her position three houses down, she had a clear view of the backyard. She'd asked Margaret to close the curtains in the front of the house and was staked out to see if Harry would show up. Mallory hoped that by not being able to see into the front of the house, Harry would move to the back.

So far, nothing. She'd sat through dinner, sat through the men talking seriously as the women sat around the living room chatting, and now she wanted to go home. Looking at Reid hurt too much. But Allegra was like family to her, and she would do whatever it took to put Harry Daniels away. Or she'd die protecting her. She felt her gun at the small of her back. The Simpsons were more of a family to her than her own stuffy parents.

She looked through the large azalea bush and scanned the trees, looking for Harry. Nothing. She opened her bag and put her binoculars away. She pulled out the thermal imaging camera and turned it on. She huddled in her leather jacket and let her hands warm up in the jacket pocket as it calibrated.

Mallory picked it up and started her thermal scan. She saw squirrels and birds in the trees, a deer, and a couple of cats. The fire the men were standing by burned red, orange, and yellow. She scanned behind them into the small wooded area and froze. Behind a large tree she caught glimpses of some greens and blues. Someone was there. She set the imager down and picked up the binoculars. He must be camouflaged; she couldn't see him at all. But now she knew where he was.

She set the binoculars down and checked her gun before crawling along the hedgerow into the thinly wooded area behind the houses. She'd been trained by the best and didn't make a sound as she made her way toward her target. Mallory's breathing was controlled. Her grip on her gun was confident as she approached him from behind.

He was covered in woods-themed camouflage. A hoodie covered his head and he wore dark gloves on his hands. No wonder he barely showed up on her thermal imager. Mallory took a shooter's stance and clicked off the safety of the gun. He whirled at the sound and stared at her from underneath his hoodie.

"Put your hands up, Harry," she said calmly as she stared into the shadows of his face.

All she saw in the dark were his lips pulling back into a half-smile, half-snarl. Her instincts were to shoot, but she didn't know if he was armed so she held back and braced herself for the hit she knew was coming. He lunged at the same time she did. Their bodies tangled in the air before falling to the ground. Mallory let out a quick breath of air to empty her lungs.

The impact sent her gun to the leaf-covered ground, but she didn't have time to worry about that. He landed on top of her, and Mallory was quick to shift her hips and roll them until she was on top of him. She moved her arms to block the hits coming at her head. When she reached for him, his leg came up and hooked around her. He twisted and she fell to his side. He was on top of her then, his hand in her hair as he pulled her head up toward him in order to smash it into the ground.

Mallory didn't worry. She'd been in worse situations that this. She looked up at him and smiled. He faltered, and she slammed her fist onto the side of his head. He fell sideways with the impact, and she made her move. She leapt up and lashed out with a kick of her combat boots to his midsection. She heard a whoosh of air as he absorbed the kick.

He reached for her and grabbed her foot. Mallory slammed her other boot down on his hand. He let out a yowl of pain and a very nasty curse.

"It's over," Mallory told him as she stared down at him. She saw the men from the fire running toward them.

"It's not over until Allegra is mine," he snarled before bursting upward and taking her down with a football tackle.

He brought his hand back and smashed it into her face. She felt heat and pain burst around her eye. She reached for him then, but he was already leaping off her. She rolled over, shook the stars from her vision, and took off after him. She ignored Reid's calls and ran as fast as she could after Harry. He was right ahead of her as they ran through the trees, jumped over fallen branches, and then burst onto a major intersection.

Her feet pounded the concrete as she chased after him. He tore down an alley next to a bakery, and she blindly charged around the corner. That was her mistake. A metal garbage can swung right at her head. She only had a split second to raise her arms in defense, but it was enough to take her down hard.

"There's nothing you can do to stop me from making Allegra mine. It's our fate, and you can't fight it." He smirked down at her. With a swift kick to her stomach, he left her dragging in breaths of air as he hopped a chain-link fence and disappeared.

"Mallory!" Reid was the first to find her. Drake, Logan, and Finn were only steps behind. Reid stopped, but the other three continued down the alley and over the fence.

Mallory let loose a string of curse words that would have her mother suffering a fit of the vapors. She slammed her hand on the cold asphalt and slowly rocked back onto her knees.

"Are you okay?" Reid asked as he bent next to her. She looked up as he sucked in a breath and made her curses pale in comparison. "We need to get you to the hospital. Your eye is almost swollen shut, and there's a nasty bump on your head."

Mallory waited for the world to stop spinning. She felt her eyes and the bump on her head. "Nah. I'm okay."

"You must have a head injury because you just got the crap beaten out of you, and you're not even complaining about breaking a nail."

Mallory rolled her one good eye. "You'll never let me forget I was a socialite, will you? Well, guess what? I've been a lot worse off than this before and lived. You don't know anything about me anymore, Reid, because you've never bothered to look."

Reid stood up and looked down at her. She hated it. The way he looked at her without seeing the real her. He'd never let her explain. Well, it didn't matter. He didn't matter, she told herself, even if her heart was calling her a liar.

"Here are the guys," Reid said distantly as he took his eyes from her. "Did you find him?"

"No," Finn said as a bead of sweat dripped down his forehead. "He was gone by the time we reached the end of the alley. Holy crap, Mallory!"

Mallory waved him off as she wobbled to stand. Her hand rested on the brick wall of the bakery. "I'm fine."

"You need to get that checked out," Drake said as he came to put an arm around her.

Mallory shrugged him off. She was not going to look weak in front of the man who stomped on her heart. "I have a guy I can call. I'm more worried about Allegra."

Finn listened to what Mallory saw and what Harry said. His blood ran cold. She wasn't safe anywhere. He would find her.

"We need to find someplace for Allegra to stay that he

can't easily sneak into."

"Name any building. We'll buy it, post guards everywhere," Reid said sharply.

"I don't think that will work. I think that's what he would expect us to do. He's smart. He'll just study it until he finds the weak spot and then slip in. We need to think of something different."

"I have an idea," Finn said quietly. When everyone looked at him, he said the last thing he wanted to. "I can take her to my mom's house."

"How is that safer than a locked-down building?" Reid asked skeptically.

"Sadly, my old neighborhood is probably more armed than your bodyguards, and they know every single person for blocks. It would be very hard to sneak into the place. There are people up all night, and when they finally go to bed, the old guard come out to walk or keep an eye out their windows." He knew she'd be safe there, but would she be able to look past the crime, drugs, and guns to see the good people there among the bad? And more importantly, what would his mom and his friends think of sweet little Allegra Simpson?

Chapter Seventeen

Allegra couldn't get warm. She snuggled into her coat as Finn turned the heat on full blast. She had freaked out when the men got back to the house and told her what had happened. Mallory was hurt, and it was her fault. It all felt like her fault again. She could kill Harry if she found him.

Finn drove her into a part of town she'd never been in before. It looked very much like the neighborhood she'd grown up in. People sat on the porches in the dark as they drank beer or talked, a couple of older men played chess at a large window so they could watch the comings and goings, and there were nice houses next to the rundown ones. The only difference was the gang signs painted on some of the corners.

"Is this where you grew up?" Allegra asked as she looked at the houses they were passing.

"Yes," was all Finn said. She heard the tension in his voice and wondered why he didn't want her here.

"Do you not want to introduce me to your mother?"

Finn had promised she could say or ask anything. She didn't feel like being quiet anymore. "Um. It's not really that," Finn stammered.

"Then what is it? You're so tense."

"What do you think of the neighborhood?" Finn asked

instead.

Allegra looked out the window and watched a drug deal go down. She watched an older lady sweeping her porch and then taking her broom to ream the drug dealer. She smacked him with the broom, and the boy looked thoroughly chastised.

Allegra shrugged her shoulders. "It kind of reminds me of where I grew up—drug deals and all." Allegra remembered her mother standing vigilantly at the end of their cracked driveway, lecturing a young man who was selling pot on the corner. She couldn't imagine her mom hitting someone with a broom, but she did bribe him with cookies.

"Really?" Finn looked surprised.

"Yeah. You knew I didn't grow up in a rich neighborhood. There was prostitution, drugs, thefts—but mixed in were some really good people. It's why my dad worked so hard. He wanted to get us out of there. I'm sure it's similar to what you're doing."

Finn just stared at her as he sat at a stop sign. "I've been so stupid. I thought you would see this and think I wasn't good enough."

"Don't be silly. I can hotwire a car better than half the people on this street." Finn's eyes grew wide and Allegra just shrugged. "Mom said to make nice with the neighbors. The neighbors owned a chop shop."

Finn broke out in laughter, and Allegra smiled at him. She felt the tension dissipate. "You'll fit in perfectly then." He pressed on the gas and a few minutes later pulled to a stop in front of a perfect little cottage house. Different-colored mums were growing in pots, and there wasn't a weed in sight.

"This is it," Finn told her. "My mom doesn't know

we're coming."

"What? I'm meeting your mom for the first time, and she doesn't even know we're coming? Finn, it's almost eleven at night, and the house is dark. We're not only coming unannounced, we're waking her up!"

"It's not a big deal. I usually stop by late and crash here if I need to."

"Yeah, but not with a woman . . . at least I hope not with women."

Finn chuckled. "No, you're the only woman worth meeting my mom."

"And you're choosing to introduce her on what's been a terrifying night by waking her up and asking her to put me up. Great. I'll make a wonderful first impression."

The rap at her window made her jump. She looked at a man a few years older than her staring in at them with a smile on his face. Allegra rolled down the window. "Hi, strange man knocking at my window. Can I ask you a question?"

The man with the tattoos around his neck looked amused. "Sure."

"Would you introduce your girlfriend who's running from a dangerous stalker to your mother in the middle of the night without giving her a heads-up?"

The man continued to look amused as he looked between Finn and Allegra, then he just laughed. "Finn, man. What a dick move to pull on your girl."

Allegra smiled. "Oh, you're friends with Finn. Hi, I'm Allegra."

"A beautiful name for a beautiful woman. I'm Terrell, and I've known Finn since he was just a kid. Now, what's this about some man stalking you?"

Allegra liked Terrell. She knew what some of those

tattoos meant, but he seemed nice enough. If he was friends with Finn, then she'd give him a chance. Finn got out of the car and did some handshake thingy with Terrell and then opened her door for her.

"Come on down to my place. The boys are there and you can tell us what's going on."

Allegra noticed faces in windows looking out at her. She did stick out from the number of people out on the street this late at night. It would be hard for someone unknown to sneak in.

"Let me show you around," Terrell said as they walked down the cracked sidewalk. "This street is good. Everyone will know you're Finn's woman in a couple minutes. But, don't go past that stop sign. That house there, she has the best snacks. The old man looking out his window at you is old school, but he's harmless."

"Are you harmless?" Allegra asked.

"To friends. But don't confuse me with a nice guy. Speaking of which, here are the boys that run this street. This is Finn's woman, Allegra." A bunch of guys raised their chins quickly, and a couple actually said hello. "They're in trouble. Go ahead, Finn, what's up?"

Allegra sat back and let Finn tell the story. She kept her eyes moving up and down the street. She wondered if Harry was out there watching. Finn finished with that night's events.

"That's some serious shit," Terrell said as his boys nodded their heads in agreement.

"What's this guy look like?"

Allegra told them and mentioned his tendency to cover his face with a hoodie and possibly something under it.

"Rolls, go tell the others to be on the lookout for this guy. If we find him, then we'll take care of it for you."

Allegra smiled sweetly at him. "Thank you. But . . . before you do anything, if you could bring him by so I could kick him in the balls and hand him over to the FBI, I'll be very appreciative."

Terrell chuckled. "You've got a good one here, Finn. We all knew you'd make something of yourself, and now you've got yourself a fine woman."

"I do. Better than I deserve."

"Isn't that always the case? But now you better take her home to meet your ma. We'll take care of things out here."

Allegra reached out and placed her hand on his large muscled arm. "Thank you, Terrell. And all of you."

"Guys, walk Allegra back to the car and help her get her things. I want a moment with Finn."

"Shall we, gentlemen," Allegra said saucily and a couple of them actually smiled at her.

Finn waited to see what Terrell needed. "This is some crazy stuff you're involved in. We'll keep an eye open and let you know what we hear."

"Thanks, I appreciate it."

"Sure thing. We're family." Terrell looked back to where Allegra was walking back to the car. "She's nice, but I don't think she'll be able to take care of herself. Growing up in a life of privilege doesn't prepare you for a battle. And dealing with this stalker is going to be a battle."

"Don't underestimate her. There's courage and strength under that layer of kindness. And she didn't grow up in a life of privilege. She grew up in the neighborhood by the train tracks on the west side of town."

"Damn. That's a bad neighborhood. Maybe she can take care of herself."

Finn made his way back to the car and helped Allegra carry her bag up the front steps of the house he had grown up in. He fished out his key and opened the door.

"Mom!" he called out as he locked the door.

Up the narrow stairs a light came on. "Finn, honey, is that you?"

"Yes, Mom. I'm here for the night, and I brought someone for you to meet."

"At midnight? Is he wanted?"

"In a way," Allegra called out. He heard his mother's footsteps freeze. "And I'm sorry, I didn't realize he failed to tell you we were coming."

"Thanks for throwing me under the bus," Finn whispered to Allegra.

She shrugged. "I'll do whatever it takes to get your mom to like me, and I'm not sorry for it."

Finn didn't stop the grin that grew on his face. There was the Allegra he knew was fighting to break free. "That's my girl," he whispered before facing back up the stairs. He heard his mother frantically running around her room.

"Yeah, sorry about introducing you to the woman I love with no warning. Allegra just informed me I shouldn't have done that."

His mom's head poked out the door at the top of the stairs. "Love?"

"That's right."

"Oh goodness gracious, my baby's in love," Mrs. Williams flew down the stairs with her dressing gown haphazardly buttoned. She pushed past Finn and grabbed Allegra's hands. "Let me just take a look at you. You're lovely!"

Allegra blushed. "It's so nice to meet you, Mrs. Williams."

"Oh no, dear. You can call me Willa. Everyone does, and hopefully someday I can be 'Mother' to you."

Allegra giggled, and Finn wished the floor would open and swallow him up.

"Have you been talking to my mother?"

His mom beamed a smile at Allegra and patted her hands. "Mothers' intuition. But, what's the matter? Why are you here so late at night?"

Finn told his mother a less scary version of what he told Terrell. By the end of the story, his mom patted Allegra's hands once again, excused herself, and a minute later came back with her shotgun named Freddy.

"Freddy and I will look out for you. Don't you worry. I'll shoot his little pecker off if he dares shows his face in our neighborhood. Now, Finn, why don't you take her to your room? Then grab a pillow and blanket for yourself to make a bed on the couch down here."

Finn looked at the lumpy couch and cringed. "The couch? Seriously. I'm thirty-four years old." His mother leveled a glare at him that made him feel like a teenager again. "Yes, ma'am."

He heard Allegra trying to stop laughing next to him. Not that he didn't respect his mother's wishes, but he just felt better with Allegra in his arms at night. Although, the thought of showing her his room was a little scary. As he led her up the stairs, he wondered how he could try to play it off as cool. There was no hope. She was going to know how lame he was.

"About my room," Finn started as he tried to think of a way to explain that his mother had not changed a thing about it since he was in high school. "It's, um, retro?"

Allegra looked back at him as she climbed the stairs. "Retro? What does that mean?"

"It's a study in late nineties coolness. Very hip now." Finn opened the door next to his mother's room and watched Allegra soak in all that made the 1990s so great. A Kobe Bryant poster covered one small wall. A big *A* for the Atlanta Braves-themed comforter set drew her attention next. A picture of him and his friends sat on a chest. He thought about tackling Allegra onto the bed before she could pick the photo up but decided to get this nightmare over with.

Allegra held it and snickered. "Are those athletic shorts? They touch the top of your white Adidas shoes. I didn't know you played soccer. And wow, nice gold necklace."

"It was the nineties, okay? I'm sure your yearbook picture wouldn't be any better."

"How did those shorts stay on?"

"I had to pull them up quite often. But I was very cool."

"I'm sure you thought you were. Nice, no smile, I'm-too-cool-for-pictures look you have going on there."

Finn came up behind Allegra and wrapped his arms around her. He kissed her neck seductively. When he felt her relax into him, he snatched the picture from her hands. "No more evidence for you. Next time I see your mom I'm going to get some dirt on you."

"Finn! I'm sure Allegra is getting tired," his mother called up from downstairs.

"I'm kinda scared to introduce our mothers. We'll be married before we know it."

Finn's breathing stopped. Was Allegra thinking about marriage? He hadn't even hoped that his dream would come true. He was still battling his self-confidence and to hear the word *marriage* come out her mouth sent his heart into a tailspin.

He forced a chuckle out. "Right. Um, goodnight. I'll be downstairs if you need anything." Finn bent awkwardly and gave her a peck on the cheek. As he walked downstairs, he let out a breath and chided himself. He was usually so cool with women. What was wrong with him? Shoot, he'd once given a woman an orgasm just by whispering in her ear. Now he couldn't say the right thing to the woman he loved to save his life. Finn flopped on the couch and stared up at the ceiling. He needed to find some game.

Allegra stared at the empty door. What had happened? Finn had brought marriage up before, or at least things that sounded like it. But when she joked about it, he literally ran out the door. Dammit. She shouldn't have said anything. What a horrible joke to make. Maybe he thought she meant she didn't want to be married to him.

She fell back onto the bed and stared at the ceiling. It was too soon to think about marriage. She shouldn't push or even bring it up. Finn would do that when he was ready. But, in her heart, she knew it was what she wanted all along. Sometimes it's just different. Her sisters had all said that, and now it made sense. She felt she could be herself with Finn. She could take risks, not be "made-up" all the time, and not be afraid to speak up. She could be herself.

No, she was in love with Finn and wasn't ashamed of it. They completed each other. They gave each other strength and encouragement to try new things and were there to catch each other if they fell. That was love. They were a couple. Sure, hot sex was a great perk, but hot sex didn't make a marriage. Hot sex with love, support, and respect—*that* made a marriage.

Allegra listened to the house. It was quiet. She tiptoed to the door. She was tired of hiding what she wanted. She'd always hidden how she really felt and answered questions diplomatically. No more. Finn had wanted no more secrets; well, he was going to get just that.

Allegra turned the handle so slowly the latch didn't make a sound. She opened the door enough to poke her head out. Willa had her door open an inch, but no light came from her room. She listened, and all she heard was a soft snore. Allegra opened the door a little wider and walked slowly out into the hall. She held her breath as she tiptoed past Willa's door and down the stairs.

"What's the matter?" Finn whispered the second her feet touched the bottom of the stairs. He stood with the shotgun in his hands as he looked into the shadows up the stairs.

"I needed to talk to you," Allegra whispered. She glanced upstairs and hoped they didn't get busted before she could tell Finn everything.

Finn relaxed and motioned for her to follow him into the kitchen. "What's going on?"

"I love you, and I want to marry you," Allegra blurted out. Finn's eyes widened, and Allegra wanted to bang her head against the refrigerator. That was not how she thought this would go.

Finn smiled so sexily that Allegra forgot to be embarrassed. "Are you proposing to me?"

"Um, I don't know." She had never thought about proposing to him. She'd always imagined a really romantic fairy-tale proposal. But if anything, she'd learned recently fairy tales were just that, tales. Real life was a lot more complicated, and a lot more rewarding.

Finn stepped forward and set his hands on her hips. He waited until she looked up at him before he said anything. "I want to marry you, too. However, I have a favor to ask you."

"Okay." Allegra felt her heart start beating triple time.

"I've been dreaming of asking you to marry me. I want to do the whole romantic gesture, down-on-one-knee thing. Will you let me do that?"

Oh gosh, yes. The feelings rushing through her were so much better than a fairy tale. "That's so sweet. Yes! I didn't mean to have it sound like a proposal; it's just that you said no secrets, and I was afraid I messed up when I mentioned marriage and if it wasn't something you wanted then . . ."

"Sweetheart, I want it more than I can ever tell you. Do you know how happy you've made me? I never dreamed a woman as amazing as you would even give me the time of day. To hear you say you love me and want to marry me—it makes me feel as if I could do anything."

"We're lucky, aren't we?" Allegra asked as she laid her head against his chest.

"Yes, we are. Too many people would just give up, given the hardships we've endured. We've shared the burden together and grown even closer."

"Finn, is everything okay down there?" his mother called out. Allegra felt her face turn red. They'd just been busted.

"Everything is fine, Mom," Finn called back and gave a quick eye roll that had Allegra covering her mouth so Willa couldn't hear her laughing.

"I just needed something to drink. I'm on my way up now, Willa," Allegra called out. "Thank you for letting me talk to you tonight," Allegra whispered to Finn before she placed a gentle kiss on his lips. She lingered there, enjoying the feeling of him close to her.

"You can talk to me about anything. And I'm glad you did, too. Goodnight, Allegra."

"Goodnight, Finn." Allegra practically bounded up the stairs. There was no way she'd be able to hide the huge smile on her face tomorrow at work.

He slammed his hand against the steering wheel. Allegra hadn't come home tonight. He started his car to head toward Finn's place. If she was there, Finn was going to pay for it. He was so close to making Allegra his. That usurper wasn't going to ruin this now.

The lights to Finn's place were off. He drove by and parked a couple of streets away. He pulled up his hoodie and stayed in the shadows as he approached the garage. Finn's car wasn't there. Where the hell was his wife?

He pulled some tools from his jacket and slid them into the backdoor lock. A minute later, there was a *click* as the lock slid open. He stepped inside Finn's house and looked around. The bed was made and there were no dirty dishes in the sink. Finn and Allegra weren't there.

In frustration he picked up a picture of Finn and an older woman who looked to be his mother and threw it against the wall. The glass shattered, and he let out a deep breath. Finn would pay for this. He looked back at the picture lying among the broken glass. Would Finn take Allegra to meet his mother? Of course he would if he thought he had a right to Allegra.

He pulled out his phone and started searching. In less than a minute he was armed with directions to Mrs. Willa Williams's address.

He drove into the neighborhood and pulled up his hoodie. There were too many eyes looking at him. It was three in morning, yet people were walking down the street and standing in groups. Lights in houses were on, and it seemed as if everyone was staring at him.

He went to turn down the street Allegra was most likely on, but a man in a similar hoodie stepped out into the street. He slammed on the brakes, and the man ambled over to his window. He couldn't be seen here. He couldn't be identified. He put his car in reverse and slammed on the gas. He'd just have to find another way to get to Allegra.

Chapter Eighteen

Finn waited for Allegra to finish getting dressed. He hadn't slept all night. His mind had been racing from their conversation. It took two hours for him to even admit to himself that marrying Allegra Simpson was a possibility. Then he spent another two hours debating if he should wait a while, or if he should just drop to one knee the second he had a ring in hand. Once he decided he needed to at least get a ring, he turned to thinking of romantic ways to propose.

A knock at the door had his mother hurrying through the kitchen. He was glad to have a moment to himself. Ever since his mother came downstairs an hour ago, she'd been shooting him funny looks and smiling at him. It was like she knew the debate going on in his head.

"Finn, it's for you," his mother called out.

Finn slid the chair back. It was probably Terrell with his end-of-the-night report. The sun was just coming up, and Terrell would be headed to bed. Finn walked to the door and was half-right. Terrell stood with a look of utter amazement as he stared at Mallory Westin in all of her full Southern-belle glory.

"You are a goddess," Terrell murmured. Finn and his mother shot a surprised look at each other and tried to hide their grins as Terrell actually blushed.

Mallory smiled at him, and he blushed deeper. "Aren't you sweet? You're just saying that because I took out two of your men."

"Hell yeah, I am. That and you look like an angel." Finn laughed at Terrell that time. His friend was a complete mess.

"Why did you take out two of Terrell's men? Are they all right?" his mother asked.

"Just seeing how safe Allegra was here," Mallory said with a shrug of a shoulder.

"She was a vision. I'm glad I didn't shoot her," Terrell said with reverence. He had it bad.

"I'm glad, too. Thank you for keeping my friends safe. One of the men I took down did mention that an unknown car with a man in a hoodie came into the neighborhood around three in the morning. When he asked the man's business, the driver took off."

"Was it Harry?" Allegra asked as she came down the stairs.

"We don't know. My guy didn't get a good look at him. But I have a car make and model. Plus he snagged part of a plate. I'll see what I can find out after I drop Allegra off at work."

"That's encouraging, right?" Finn's mom asked.

"Right. But now I'm taking Allegra to Tigo's."

"I can take her to work," Finn said. He didn't want to be separated from her for one minute.

"Sorry, but you have meetings all day out of office. Good thing you gave me your schedule, huh?" Mallory teased.

"Let me just get my things, and I'll be ready." Allegra smiled at them and turned to run upstairs.

"She might need help," Finn managed to say before

racing upstairs for a couple minutes alone with her before heading to work.

Mallory grinned as Finn hurried upstairs. There was something more comfortable between them now. It was as if their relationship was more solid. Strange, considering all the stress they were both under. But it was something the whole Simpson family had been hoping would happen for months. Margaret would be beside herself. Mallory just hoped Allegra wouldn't let Shirley plan the bachelorette party.

"So, you're in security, huh?"

Mallory turned her attention back to the man standing next to her. He was handsome in an unconventional way—built and tatted up to his neck, literally. "That's right."

"So you're like a bodyguard?"

"Sometimes. We also do security for companies and certain individuals. That's everything from evaluations of security systems, to installations of new ones, to protecting certain materials when they need to be transported. Basically a little of everything."

"If I hadn't seen you take two men out with my own eyes, I'd never believe it. What does it take to be a bodyguard?"

"Why, are you interested in applying for a job?" she asked. She doubted he would be qualified, but it was always good to keep friends in a variety of places.

"If I could work with you, then I would be."

Mallory pulled out her card and handed it to him. "Ethan is in charge of hiring. Email him your contact info and skill sets. We may not have a full-time opening, but we do hire outside help as needed."

"Thanks." Terrell took the card and stepped back as

Allegra hurried out the door. Her lips were swollen, and Mallory noticed her shirt was on backward. Mrs. Williams smacked Finn's head, so apparently she noticed, too.

"It was nice meeting y'all," Mallory told them before ushering Allegra to the car. She had a gut feeling her lead was going to pan out. She couldn't wait to track it down, but getting Allegra safely tucked into her office was priority number one.

"Allegra and Finn, K-I-S-S . . ."

"Really, Elle?" Allegra cut her older sister off.

"I-N-G. And probably doing it while they were N-A-K . . ."

"Bree!" Allegra shouted, cutting her other sister off. "Oh my gosh, you two. How old are you?"

"I distinctly remember you doing this to me. Payback is fair game, dear sister." Elle grinned, not looking the slightest bit sorry.

"Can you blame her? I mean, we've all seen him naked," Shirley said, wheeling in from the hallway. *I twerk for a living* was hanging on her walker as she came in.

Allegra turned bright red. "You all need to forget that ever happened."

"Not a chance. I tried to snap a picture, but I couldn't find my phone fast enough," Shirley said as she took a seat.

"So, I take it you all have worked out any issues? You seemed pretty upset at the other family dinner," Bree asked nosily. They were her sisters so Allegra didn't expect anything less. She'd already received a phone call from her mother so, if anything, they were behind the game.

"Yes. It was silly. We talked about it, and we're fine."

Elle nodded seriously. "That's so important. Too many silly things can be blown out of proportion. But if you just communicate, then the hardest part of a relationship is handled. It takes guts to bare your feelings. Look at our little sister all grown up," Elle teased Bree.

"What are your plans tonight? If he gets naked again, see if you can snap me a picture."

"Shirley, I am not sending you naked pictures of Finn."

"Fine, but when you get engaged I'm throwing the bachelorette party."

All three sisters looked at each other in terror. They all remembered the escorts Shirley had gotten for the last bachelorette party. Bree had been smart to get married so quickly that the sisters just had a slumber party to celebrate the night before the wedding.

"I don't know what we're doing tonight. Mallory is hunting down a lead and Mr. No Neck is babysitting me." Allegra gestured to the man sitting out in the hall.

"I wouldn't mind a picture of him naked," Shirley said as she checked him out.

"Have you signed up for one of those cougar dating sites?" Bree asked with mischief in her eyes.

"They have those? Hot diggity. If you'll excuse me, I'm going to take some sexy selfies before signing up."

The sisters watched as Shirley sprang up from her seat and hurried out the door. Then she stopped in front of Mr. No Neck and dropped something. The girls all giggled as Mr. No Neck stood up and bent over to pick it up. He didn't see Shirley pulling out her phone and taking a picture.

"Oh my gosh, I feel sorry for any site she signs up on," Elle said as they watched her roll down the hall.

Bree looked at her phone and groaned. "I have to go.

We have a new site ready to start, and I need to go do my ground-breaking thing. Do they have any idea how hard it is to shovel in high heels and a skirt?"

"Aw, but you look totally hot doing it," Allegra teased.

"That's because I'm wearing my sister's new line," Bree winked. "And hey, I'm really happy for you and Finn. He's a super-great guy, and I can see he makes you happy."

"Me too," Elle added. "It's great to see you in love. Keep us updated on how things are going."

"I will. Thank you, both." Allegra stood up and hugged her sisters. Sometimes she wanted to slam a pillow in their faces, but they were her sisters, and she knew they would be by her side through thick and thin.

"And if you do get married to Finn, please, please elope. I don't think Mom would survive another of Shirley's bachelorette parties," Elle said earnestly.

Allegra watched her sisters leave as they joked about Elle's bachelorette party. She waited until they were out of sight and went back to work. Some of her brands were in Italy for its Fashion Week. She read reports that were sent from her Italian staff and got lost in watching online videos of the shows.

Finn wrapped up his meeting at Atlanta's premier country club and headed through the bar on his way out. The place was all dark, rich wood with plush carpet. Men clustered at the bar, bragging about their golf scores or their latest business deals. This was the side of business he was having trouble getting used to. He was a no-BS kind of guy but took Elle's advice and learned how to play golf. He couldn't believe the number of deals he got over eighteen holes. It was also fascinating that the better he got at golf, the more seriously people took him.

As darkness fell over the greens, Finn found his mind finally able to concentrate on Allegra. He wanted to do something romantic for her. He wasn't ready to ask her to marry him quite yet. He still needed to get a ring and plan a proposal. But he wanted to show her he could romance her. She deserved that—to feel loved and cherished. And hopefully, she would spill something about what kind of ring she'd want.

He felt like a new man with the decision to marry her being made. But before he asked he was going to do some serious wooing. He was even considering calling Nate to discuss some ideas for after Harry was caught.

Finn smiled as he unlocked his car. If he hurried, he could call for a reservation at Allegra's favorite restaurant and pick her up at the office. His mind drifted to other romantic things he wanted to do as he picked up the phone. He couldn't wait to begin surprising her and showing her how much she meant to him.

The knock on the door surprised Allegra, but when she saw Mr. No Neck holding one of Finn's huge white boxes, she could hardly contain her excitement. Looking up, she saw the city lights brightening the Atlanta skyline, and most of the people in her office had gone home for the night.

"Do I need to check this? It was delivered to security at the front desk," Mr. No Neck told her.

"No. I know who it's from. Thank you. I won't be too much longer."

"My replacement will be here shortly so take your time. Call if you need anything." The hulk of a man headed back out to his spot overlooking the office.

Allegra couldn't wait. She tore into the box and pulled out the note. *I can't wait any longer to make you mine. Wear the dress if you love me so we can say I Do.*

Allegra's breath caught as she read the card and then pulled out a beautiful white column wedding dress from the box. It was made of satin with pearl beading along the sweetheart neckline and under the bust. Under the dress were matching high heels. When Finn said he wanted to make a statement, boy, did he know how to do it!

A low whistle caused Allegra to jerk her head up from looking at the dress. "Shirley, you scared me to death."

"Is that what I think it is?" she asked as she scooted forward to get a closer look at the dress.

"Yes." Allegra's smile covered her whole face. "Finn wants me to elope with him right now."

"But, I wanted to throw you a bachelorette party. I had even called our friend Aiden to see what his schedule was like. I guess being a witness to the wedding will have to do."

Allegra's smile fell. "Witness?" Finn hadn't said anything about a witness in his note.

"Sure, you should have someone there, you know. Otherwise it's the judge and a couple of people of no importance to you. You should have someone there who loves you."

Allegra looked at Shirley's eyes filled with such love that she couldn't say no. Her mother would be madder than a hornet, but she loved Finn, and if that's what he wanted, then she would happily go. They could always have a big family reception. Or, knowing Finn, she was pretty sure this was a setup. She was sure when she arrived at the location, all her family would already be there. After all, they all made a point to call her today and tell her how much they loved Finn and how happy they were for her. They all talked as if marriage were inevitable. Oh, Finn! She couldn't wait to marry him.

"Sure, Shirley. I'd love for you to escort me," Allegra said with a wink. She wouldn't let on she'd figured out Finn's plan. If her family wanted to help him with the surprise, so be it. "Give me just a minute to get ready."

Mallory stood in the shadows of the woods outside Atlanta with Agent Hectoria. The forensic crews carefully dug dirt away from the detection site illuminated by portable lights. A hand wrapped in plastic was already exposed where Axe, the golden retriever, had started digging while on a hike with his owners.

When the young couple went to pull Axe away, they discovered the hand and called the police. Mallory's contact had called her, and she'd called Agent Hectoria.

"Okay, I'm here. But I don't see why this is important to Miss Simpson's case." Agent Hectoria stood, her hand resting on her gun, and watched the excavation.

Mallory's eyes didn't leave the increasingly exposed body. "I got a tip from Finn's neighborhood. I followed it up and ran the partial plate they saw. The car was reported stolen from an apartment complex near here. That's too much of a coincidence for me."

"That's a pretty big leap, Miss Westin."

"Maybe, but I have a gut feeling about this."

"I guess we'll find out."

Mallory and Agent Hectoria stepped forward as the dirt was brushed away from the head. The body hadn't been buried too deeply, and the forensic team was ready to open the plastic.

"I'm hoping the body will be in good enough shape for

an identification. It's been pretty cold at night. That'll slow decomp," the forensic lead told them as he reached for a knife.

He cut the duct tape holding the plastic closed and put it in an evidence bag. Their lab techs would have a field day getting fibers and samples from it. They pulled back the plastic and Mallory stepped forward.

"Shit," Mallory cursed.

"But . . . that's Harry Daniels," Agent Hectoria gasped as she held up a picture of him next to the decomposing body. "Then who has been stalking Allegra Simpson?"

Chapter Nineteen

"Oh, honey, you look beautiful!" Shirley dabbed at the tears in her eyes as Allegra did a twirl. The two women had been ensconced in Allegra's bathroom for the last thirty minutes getting dressed for her surprise wedding.

"Thank you. I'm so glad you're here with me, Shirley." Allegra smiled at the woman who was as close to her as a grandmother could be. It was sweet of Finn to send her. She was sure her mother was running around like a madwoman decorating and organizing while Reid, Drake, and Logan were probably toasting Finn in their tuxedos.

The women stepped out of the large bathroom and hurried to grab their purses. Allegra opened the door, and Shirley wheeled her way out into the hall. Nervous energy raced through her as she pressed the elevator button. She couldn't seem to stop talking. Maybe if she had, she would have noticed her bodyguard missing.

Mallory pulled out her phone and dialed the guard on duty. She paced back and forth as her heart pounded. The phone rang and finally went to voicemail. Mallory cursed again and dialed Allegra. The phone went straight to voicemail.

"Miss Westin!" Agent Hectoria called out from where Harry Daniels lay uncovered now.

"I can't get a hold of my man watching Allegra. Allegra's not answering her phone either," Mallory told her as she hurried over. She cringed when she saw what Agent Hectoria surely wanted.

"We have the cause of death," Agent Hectoria said grimly.

Mallory felt the blood drain from her face. Harry Daniel's throat had been slit. "I have to get to Simpson Global."

"I'm calling all of the agencies now. I'll have people sent to her home and Mr. Williams's home."

Mallory didn't bother to thank Agent Hectoria; she was already running for her car. Her gut had been right about Harry Daniels's disappearance, but now she had wished it hadn't been.

Finn grinned to himself as he rode the elevator up to Allegra's office. He had a dinner reservation at Allegra's favorite restaurant, a vase bursting with purple dendrobium orchids, and all the love he wanted to shower her with.

The elevator doors opened, and he frowned. The lights on the floor were off, and her office door was closed. It was hard to make out the furniture except for the glowing light from an Exit sign at the far end of the room. He stepped forward and set the flowers down on her bodyguard's chair. Reaching for his phone, he dialed her number.

Hi, you've reached Allegra Simpson . . .

The elevator dinged, and Finn tensed. Something was very wrong. His instincts kicked in, and he ducked down behind her secretary's desk. There were no further sounds, which Finn thought was strange. He held his breath as he listened, but he didn't hear footsteps or even breathing. It was like no one was there.

Finn was about to stand up when a dirty boot came into view. He counted to three in his mind. Every muscle was tense, waiting to explode at his command. He lunged. His arms wrapped around the intruder in all black, propelling them down to the floor. They fought for control in the dark hallway as they rolled on the floor. Punches were thrown and kicks connected as he fought blindly with the person with a baseball cap pulled down over his head. The intruder landed a punch on his chin that caused him to see stars, but he countered by landing an elbow to the side of his head before the intruder's red painted nails reached for his throat. His eyes widened, and something clicked in his mind. The person straddling him had red nails.

"Mallory?" he choked out as he grabbed at the hand tightening around his throat.

"Finn?" The fingers instantly released, and she used her other hand to rip off her baseball cap. Her blond hair tumbled out. "What are you doing here?"

"I came to pick up Allegra, but she's not here. What are you doing here dressed like that?"

"I was dressed for recon. My hair tends to be noticeable so I had to cover it. Finn, I found Harry Daniels."

"Thank goodness. Is he in jail?" Finn's body relaxed as he looked up at Mallory still sitting on him.

"Finn, he's dead. His throat was slit about two weeks ago."

"What? That doesn't make sense."

Mallory stood up and held out her hand for him. "It's not Harry who is stalking Allegra. I'm here because I can't find her. I was hoping she was with you, but her phone goes to voicemail, and I can't get in touch with my man watching her. The guard who went off duty an hour ago said his replacement relieved him, and he left as scheduled."

"Then who is stalking her?" Finn's head spun as he tried to understand what Mallory was saying.

"We don't know. We don't even have a lead. And now we can't find Allegra. He has her, Finn. I can feel it."

"No. There has to be something. What did your guard say?" Finn tried to control the anger and fear rushing through his body. He pushed aside the voice that told him this was his fault. If he'd only been here . . .

"That she was working all day. Her sisters all visited her, along with Shirley. She didn't seem upset. In fact, he said she couldn't stop smiling all day. Especially after she got the gift you sent her."

Finn froze. "I didn't send her a gift."

They both looked toward the dark office. Finn strode forward and went to open the door, but it was locked. He shot his arm out and moved Mallory aside. Lifting his leg he slammed his foot next to the lock. The doorframe shattered and the door was flung open.

They hurried inside and stopped to stare at the white box on the table. "See, just like all your other gifts," Mallory said as she pointed to the empty box.

"Mallory, I've never sent Allegra a gift."

Mallory met his eyes, and they both knew in that instant the danger Allegra was in. "Okay, let me think. Allegra said you sent white silk lingerie, a white blouse, pearls—"

Finn just shook his head. "No. I've never done that. Dammit!" Finn slammed his hand on the desk. "She asked me about them. She showed them off to me, and I had no idea."

"Wait," Mallory held up her hand, and Finn watched as she closed her eyes, trying to remember something. "The blouse. I saw it. I just have to remember the label. It was expensive . . ."

Mallory whipped out her cell phone. "Agent. Allegra has been receiving gifts from the stalker. She thought they were from Finn, but I'm with Finn and it wasn't him. But I have an idea. Put me through to the person at her house."

"What is it?" Finn asked.

"The blouse. If I know who made it, I can track where it's sold. Maybe we can get surveillance on who bought it."

Hope surged, but Finn didn't want to get too excited.

"A white blouse. Silk, V-neck," Mallory was saying in the phone. "Silk, you know, a soft, sexy material." Mallory huffed. "Yes, buttons up the front. Okay, thank you."

"They found it?"

"Yes, and I know exactly where he got it. It's local. There's a small shop that sells that brand. Let me find the owners . . ." Mallory sat in front of Allegra's computer and booted it up.

Finn pulled out his phone and dialed the only people he knew who might have an idea of who owned that store. "David, it's Finn. Allegra has been taken. It wasn't Harry. He's dead. Our one clue is a silk blouse from Scarlett's." Finn told him the brand and waited as David and Josh talked.

"The owners are Julie and Taggart Milhouse. Their daughter, Phoebe, works there as a sales clerk. I'll call them now and have them meet you at the store."

Finn didn't even have a chance to thank them before the phone disconnected. "David and Josh came through. He's getting the owners to meet us there."

Mallory let out a breath. "Let's go," she said.

Finn and Mallory hurried out the door, but something caught Finn's eye. "Wait." Finn looked down the dark corridor and wondered what it was that seemed off.

"What is it?"

"The bathrooms. The light to the women's room is on. See, you can see the thin line of light under the door. But the men's room is completely dark."

They inched forward and stopped at the men's door. Mallory stood to one side and Finn on the other. With a nod of her head, Finn slammed the door open and flipped the light on as Mallory knelt on one knee with her gun at the ready aimed into the bathroom.

"No!" Mallory screamed as she crawled forward.

Finn swallowed hard as he looked at the bodyguard with his throat cut. Blood was pooled all around his limp body. "Mallory," Finn whispered as he put his hand on her shoulder, trying to stop her.

Mallory shrugged him off as she sat in the blood and held her man's head in her lap. "He had a wife and three children," Mallory said so softly he almost didn't hear it. Tears fell from her large blue eyes and her arms wrapped around his body. Mallory sniffled and then froze. She leaned closer to his head and sniffed again.

"What is it?"

"Chloroform. Check the trash can."

Finn ripped the metal top from the trashcan. Right on top was a cloth. He didn't pick it up, but leaned forward and sniffed it. "Smells slightly sweet."

"Don't touch it." Mallory leaned forward and whispered something to her fallen man. She slid his head slowly from her lap and back onto the ground. She stood then, blood soaking her legs as she walked forward and grabbed a handful of paper towels.

Her features were set as she washed her hands and wiped them on the towels. She used the extra towels to run over her legs and shoes. She took a deep breath and then sent a series of texts as she walked out the bathroom door and headed to the elevator. "My men will be here shortly to watch over him. I'll notify his wife as soon as I find Allegra. I'll also see if Agent Hectoria can get Allegra's car company to search her GPS and see if we can find her that way, too. We'll find her." *If she's still alive* was left unsaid.

Allegra could barely contain her excitement as she drove into the old industrial part of Atlanta. Her GPS took her to Lexington Centre, and Shirley did a great acting job as they looked to find the right address.

"Are you sure about this, dear?" Shirley asked as she looked out the window.

"Look! There it is. Oh, how pretty." The building was decorated with white paper lanterns in the parking lot, and more lined the sidewalk of the old brick building.

"It's lovely," Shirley murmured as she looked around.

"Are you all right?" Allegra asked. Shirley seemed off. Was she afraid of blowing the surprise?

"I'm fine, I'm just surprised. This doesn't seem like something Finn would do."

"What do you think Finn would do?"

"He's so close to your family; I just thought he'd do something with them."

Allegra shot her a wink. "Maybe he has."

"Well, let's find out." Shirley opened the door, and Allegra went to help her out. She opened the trunk and pulled out her walker.

Allegra looked up at the building and tried not to run

inside to see Finn. No, they would enter, and she'd pretend to be surprised when all her family was standing there. Allegra walked slowly beside Shirley. The sound of music floated outside the wooden doors. She smiled and took it all in. She pictured Finn on the other side of the doors with the glow of candles to light the ceremony. It was so romantic she had to remind herself not to rush inside and leave Shirley behind.

Finally, they approached the partially open door. She grabbed the large handle and pulled the heavy door all the way open. Allegra stepped inside and gasped. White roses lined an aisle mixed with paper lanterns. White satin bows and roses covered an arch on a raised platform wrapped in white satin. Large candelabras filled with glowing candles stood on both ends, highlighting where she and Finn would say their vows.

She stepped forward, unaware that Shirley was walking in behind her. Where was her family? The door shut behind them with a loud slam. She looked behind her; Shirley stood with a frown on her face. A shiver of anxiety ran through Allegra. This was wrong, so wrong. She didn't know why, but her mind yelled at her to leave.

"Let's go outside and call Finn," Allegra whispered to Shirley. Shirley gave a quick nod and reached for the door.

"It's not opening," Shirley said with a hint of panic to her voice.

"Ah, the bride has arrived! Stunning, simply stunning, my love."

Allegra's eyes widened at the sound of the deep voice coming from the altar. Slowly she turned around and looked at the man standing in an impeccably tailored tuxedo.

"You?" she gasped.

Chapter Twenty

The lights to Scarlett's were already on when Finn and Mallory arrived. They hadn't said a word the entire time Mallory sped through town in her sports car. Five figures were waiting impatiently at the entrance to the luxury boutique.

"David, Josh, what are you doing here?" Finn asked.

"Ohmygod," Josh rushed out as he stared wide-eyed at the drying blood on Mallory. "Allegra?"

Mallory shook her head, and the group let out a breath and took the hint not to ask any more questions.

"This is Taggert and his wife, Julie," David cut in as he introduced the older couple standing nervously in front of them. "And this is their daughter, Phoebe. She works at the counter most days."

"Thanks for coming in," Finn said, trying to hide the fear from his voice.

Phoebe looked concerned as she crossed her arms under her large breasts. "Of course, but I don't understand what we can do to help find Miss Simpson."

"About eight to ten days ago did you sell a Champlain white silk blouse to a man?" Mallory asked, her voice completely void of emotion.

Julie looked around the store and then walked to the rack in the middle of the shop. She took something off the rack and then held it up. "This one?"

Mallory glanced quickly at it and nodded. Phoebe looked over at it, and Finn could see her going through all her sales in her mind. She sucked in a breath.

"Yes!"

Finn's heart pounded. "Did he pay with a credit card?"

"No. Cash."

"Did you get a name?" Mallory asked.

"No."

"What did he look like?" Mallory stepped forward, never breaking eye contact with Phoebe.

"Tall, but not as tall as you," Phoebe nodded to Finn. "Caucasian, handsome, brown hair that was styled . . . that's all I remember. But, it was only ten days ago. We may have him on our security camera. It loops every two weeks."

"That's right," Taggert said as he pulled his keys from his pocket. "The security system is in the office."

The group got ready to go into the back when blue and red lights flashed through the window. Finn turned around and saw Agent Hectoria jump out of her car and hurry toward them.

"What do you have?" she asked in a clipped tone similar to Mallory's.

"Security camera, we might have him."

"Agent Hectoria, FBI," she said to the Milhouses.

Taggert gave her a nod. "This way."

The group followed him into the back and waited impatiently as he found the key to unlock his office. They crammed inside it and stood waiting again as he searched for the key to the security panel. Finn tried not to rip the keys from his shaky hand and find the damn thing himself.

"Here it is," Taggert said as he inserted the key. He

pulled the panel open and Mallory pushed him aside.

She scanned the system and pulled up the digital video. She started it at the beginning of the loop. "Phoebe, come here. Tell me when you see him."

Phoebe stepped forward, and they stood watching the days fast-forward by. Man after man and woman after woman came across the screen. Finn tried to keep the adrenaline in check as he watched the screen. Everyone was leaning forward trying to see something suspicious.

"Wait!" Phoebe called. "Him. That's him."

"He's not showing his face. He's avoiding the cameras," Agent Hectoria said in frustration.

"Just wait," Taggert told them. "We have visible security cameras used to deter thieves and then we have hidden ones to get their faces if they think they can get away with it. Here, press this button." He leaned forward and pressed a button and the screen split into four pictures. Two were from the cameras Finn had noticed, but two were from different angles. "One is hidden in the display case up front and the other is in a mannequin."

"There!" Julie said to the bottom left screen.

Mallory slapped the button and froze the screen. Everyone leaned forward.

"Wait, I know him!" Finn said. They'd found him.

"So do I," Mallory said at the same time as David and Josh.

"Who is it?" Agent Hectoria asked impatiently.

"Thank you, Mr. Milhouse. Please send this to the email address on my card." Mallory held out her card and then looked at Agent Hectoria who whipped out her card.

"Who is it?" Agent Hectoria asked again.

"Wait," Mallory snapped as she watched Taggert select the file and email it to both of them. She watched her phone until the email showed up. "Thank you. Please lock it back up and wait for the FBI out front. Don't touch it again. Got it?"

"Understood," Taggert closed the panel and locked it again.

Mallory turned and ushered everyone to the sidewalk.

"What's going on?" Agent Hectoria demanded.

"It's Asher Woodcroft IV," Finn cursed. "I told Allegra I didn't trust him."

"Wait, Woodcroft, of *the* Woodcroft family?" Agent Hectoria said in amazement.

Mallory slammed her fist against the hood of the agent's car. "The one and only sleazebag." She pulled up her phone and called the control center of her security firm. "Give me all the property owned by the Woodcroft family. Send it to my mobile."

Agent Hectoria shook her head slowly. "This isn't good. His family . . ."

"I know. But he's not the only one with a powerful family," Mallory said through gritted teeth. "He's already killed one of my men. I fully intend to kill him, and his family can sue me all they want. It may be better if you leave, Agent."

"I don't think so."

Mallory's phone pinged, and she looked down. "The Woodcroft holdings. There's too many—thirty at least."

"He'll want isolation," Agent Hectoria said as she stepped forward to look over Mallory's shoulder. "Look for uninhabited buildings."

Mallory sent the instruction and seconds later a new list appeared. "Six," Mallory muttered. "But he will want more than just an empty building. He'll want as much privacy as he can get. This one, it's on Peachtree. It's an old bank building. It's surrounded by shops, so that won't be it."

Finn leaned forward and looked at the address. "That one is on a residential street."

"Okay, down to four. This one," Mallory tapped at the address and a map popped up. "It's in the abandoned industrial part of town. The city is looking to take a couple of buildings by eminent domain and make it a school and park."

David snapped his fingers. "That's right. And there's talk of buying the rest of the old warehouses and turning them into luxury condos. It's one of the major city rejuvenation efforts that are being debated right now. We had looked there for our store, but the plans are still unsettled. It's a ghost town out there."

"It's on the other side of Atlanta," Mallory said as she sent a message to her office, and Agent Hectoria placed a call for backup.

"It's what, ten minutes from my old neighborhood. I know some short cuts."

"And I know someone looking for a job," Mallory said with a deadly smile.

"Asher! What are you doing here?" Allegra asked as calmly as possible. She moved to hide Shirley behind her as she kept her gaze on Asher.

He smiled so widely that Allegra wondered what was going on. He didn't look menacing, but warning bells were going off in her head. Asher stepped off the dais and sauntered down the aisle.

Asher laughed. "What am I doing here? No need to pretend anymore, love. We're to be married. I'm so glad you wore my dress. When I picked it out, I knew you would shine in it." He leaned forward and placed a lingering kiss on her cheek.

Allegra stopped breathing. All the pieces were sliding into place. Her body started to shake . . . it hadn't been Harry. She had been so very wrong.

"How sweet, my bride is nervous. I know you come to me impure, but I forgive you." His hand clasped around hers, and he tugged her forward. "But, my love, why did you bring her? This was supposed to be our moment."

Allegra looked at Shirley and felt like crying. Shirley stood frozen. Her knuckles were white where she held her walker. "Photographer," Allegra said as she turned to Asher and smiled. "I wanted to document our special day. It's so beautiful, Asher. I want to cherish it always."

Asher smiled at her. "If that is what you want, my love." He leaned forward and kissed her on the lips. Allegra fought the urge to gag. She had to protect Shirley. If that meant playing to Asher's delusions, then so be it.

"You have no idea how long I have been waiting to kiss you like that," he purred against her lips.

His hands held her hips tightly. Allegra winced in pain but slowly raised her hand to stroke his face. "Darling, why didn't you say something sooner?"

Asher's hands squeezed tighter and Allegra hissed from the pain. "I did. I asked you out, but you rejected me. *No one* rejects me," his voice no longer had a loving tone. It was demented.

"Stop!" Shirley called out. "You're hurting your bride. You don't want that, do you?"

His fingers relaxed some. "No, of course not. Now, let's be married." He smiled as if it were really their wedding day.

"Who's marrying us?" Allegra asked as Asher's hand clasped around her wrist before pulling her up the aisle.

"I am. But don't worry; it will be legal. I got Judge Schmidt to sign the marriage certificate already. He won't tell anyone he did it, or I'll make sure he gets disbarred," Asher said proudly.

Allegra shot a look over her shoulder at Shirley, who was frantically trying to unlock the door. Asher turned around to follow her gaze and squeezed so hard Allegra fell to the floor in biting pain.

"Shirley, run!"

Shirley looked back, her eyes widening as Asher ran toward her, dragging Allegra behind. She gave up trying to unlock the door. She held up her phone and snapped a picture. "Stop or I'll send it to the police." Shirley held up the phone to show the picture in a text message.

Asher slowed his steps, and Allegra ignored the pain in her wrist as she jumped up and ran to them. "Asher, honey, come on. Let's get married. It's a happy day. Just let her go, and we can get married with nothing but love surrounding us."

Allegra desperately grabbed for his arm as he approached Shirley. The look on his face was enough to cause Allegra to lose her breath. His jaw was tensed and his teeth bared in a predatory smirk. His eyes—they were cold, hard, and narrowed right at Shirley.

Mallory floored her Porsche as she shot through Atlanta. She'd left Agent Hectoria in the dust miles ago. Her phone rang, and she pressed the Bluetooth speaker.

"What do you have?"

"It's Terrell. I just got here. There's a car here. Fancy sedan. Lexus."

"Allegra," Finn and Mallory said at the same time.

"What else do you see?"

"Lights. Those paper bag things with candles inside are lining the parking lot and leading up to the door. I can hear violin music, but that's all."

"What the hell?" Finn muttered.

"Are there any windows?"

"Sure are, but they are covered in white material on the inside. I can't see in," Terrell told them. "What do you want me to do?"

"Scout the whole building. Don't try the doors, but find every entrance point you can. Tell me the entire layout when I get there. Whatever you do, don't let anyone see or hear you. I'll be there in less than ten minutes."

"Got it."

"I don't get it. What is Asher doing?" Finn asked.

"Wooing her. He's been sending her presents, just like a lover would. I just worry what will happen if Allegra rejects him."

"She already did."

"What, when?" Mallory asked as she ran a red light at ninety miles per hour.

"Seven months ago. In January, she said she was at a party, and he asked her out. She told him no. She said they'd joked about it. She didn't think he was serious. I said he wanted to sleep with her, and Allegra just laughed. She told me he wants to sleep with everyone."

"That's it. She rejected him when no one else ever had. He probably couldn't handle it and started stalking her. He's already killed two people. If Allegra rejects him again, he'll snap."

Chapter Twenty-One

Allegra pulled at his arm. "Please, love, let's get married." Her heart beat so fast she was afraid it would explode. He was going to kill Shirley if she didn't do something. She took a gulp. Forgive me, Finn, she silently begged. "Love, the faster we get married, the faster we can move onto our wedding night. I'm sorry I played hard to get. I had to see if you were man enough to catch me. And now you have me all to yourself. You've proven you're man enough to have me, to take me."

"No, Allegra. Don't do it," Shirley pleaded as tears streamed down her wrinkled face.

Allegra ran a hand down Asher's arm, drawing his attention away from Shirley. "Marry me. We can't be together until you do. Ignore her. She's just an old lady. Come on. We've waited long enough."

Allegra placed her hand on his chest and imagined it was Finn. She smiled up at him and stepped into his arms. She rose on her toes and put her lips to his. With a quick bite, she nipped at his lower lip. He moaned and wrapped his arms around her tightly. His tongue forced its way into her mouth as he took what he'd been wanting. Allegra put her hand behind her own back and waved it at Shirley. She prayed Shirley took the clue and sent the message. Allegra pulled back and looked into Asher's crazed eyes. They were filled with deranged lust as he ran his hand down her back.

Shirley sniffled. "That was so romantic. All right, I'll put the phone down." She made a show of turning it off and putting it into her purse. She looked up and smiled serenely at the couple. "Young love," she sighed.

Asher narrowed his eyes, but Allegra ran her hand down his chest. "Come on, love." She took his hand gently in hers and started toward the dais. "Did you decorate this yourself?"

"I did. Do you really like it?"

"I love it. I can't believe you did this for me. And the gifts—you're so amazing. You know, I think I knew at the New Year's party you were the one for me. It's why I made you work so hard to get me."

"I knew it was you even before then," Asher said distractedly as he kept looking over at Shirley.

"You did! Tell me, when did you fall in love with me?"

"Huh?"

"When did you fall in love with me?" Allegra looked back and forth between him and Shirley. Shirley smiled at her. She'd done it. Relief flooded her. She just had to play out this charade a little longer. Whoever was sent the picture should be able to easily identify Asher.

"Oh, love, how silly of me." Allegra laughed. "Shirley is like my grandmother; she should walk down the aisle before me. I'll stand down here. You escort her and sit her on my side. Then stand up there like you're supposed to. Do you have the 'Wedding March'?"

Asher shook his head as if clearing it. "Yes, I do. And you're right, my love. I want to watch you come down the aisle toward me."

Allegra smiled and they walked toward Shirley. Shirley held out her arm. "You'll have to help an old woman, sonny."

"Of course." Asher bowed as if he respected Shirley and offered her his arm.

Allegra smiled kindly and mouthed, "I love you" when he looked over his shoulder at her. As soon as he turned back, Allegra took a deep breath. What was she going to do? She was going to be nice, that's what. Asher was a narcissist living in his own reality. She would simply be nice, play to his ego, and hope help would arrive soon.

Mallory pushed the Bluetooth when her phone rang. "What have you got, Terrell?"

"Something weird is going on. You know that song they play at weddings when the bride walks down the aisle? Well, that music just started playing."

Finn shot a look at Mallory. Would Asher force Allegra to marry him? "Entrance points?"

"Most of the windows are barred. There's the front door, the back door, and a door by the loading dock. Those are the only options I found."

"I'm about five minutes away now. I'll meet you a block up from the building."

"Yes, ma'am."

Mallory tightened her hand on the wheel as she weaved through traffic. Finn closed his eyes and imagined what was going on inside that building. "Hurry, Mallory, this could go bad in a split second."

"Exactly what I was thinking." Mallory swerved lanes and pressed the gas when she got onto the open road.

Allegra pasted her fake smile on and batted her eyelashes. She slowly took one step at a time down the candlelit aisle

Asher had created. She was going to delay this with all she had. But no matter how slow or small her steps, they were still taking her closer to Asher.

Asher stood with his hands clasped in front of him. He smiled as if he were a devoted lover seeing his bride for the first time. Her stomach rolled at the thought of being married to him. What would he do once they said *I do*?

She reached him all too soon. He held out his hand and helped her up onto the dais. He turned her so they were looking at each other; he held her hands in his. He smiled down at her, and she saw how he loved her in his own sick way.

Asher looked down into her upturned face. She was beauty itself, and she was all his. Finally their fate was determined. He held her soft hands in his. This was his moment, the moment he'd been dreaming about. "I, Asher Edward Woodcroft IV, am here of my own free will to join in union with the love of my life, Allegra Margaret Simpson."

Asher gave an eager nod to Allegra and she repeated slowly, "I, Allegra Margaret Simpson, am here of my own free will to join in union with the love of my life, Asher Edward Woodcroft IV."

He closed his eyes and felt the pleasure run over him at her words. He'd won.

Her stomach felt as if she'd eaten rocks. Allegra tried with all her might to stop shaking. In his crazed state, Asher must have read it as wedding day nerves and simply squeezed her hands in support.

"Now we'll recite our vows. I'll go first." He took a deep breath and continued to squeeze her fingers. "Allegra,

I fell in love with you the first time I saw your picture in the newspaper. I knew at that moment you were meant for me. I learned everything I could about you. I was devastated when I found out you were dating someone else. I knew in my heart our fates were crossed. When you showed up single at the New Year's Eve party, it was the sign I was waiting for. You smiled at me, and when you shook my hand, I knew the feelings I had when I saw your picture were just the beginning of our long life together."

Asher laughed and gripped her hands to the point where she was afraid he might break a finger. Her wrist was already turning purple from where he'd grabbed her a few minutes ago.

"And then you led me on that chase. Like every good hunter, the prey is sweeter when it's captured. And captured you I have. I love you, Allegra, and I vow here, tonight, that I will take care of you. You will never have to worry about working or deciding anything again. I am here now, and I will make you my queen." Asher let out a long breath and grinned. "Okay, your turn."

"Oh, um," Allegra stammered. She shot a quick glance at Shirley who looked so still Allegra was afraid she had passed away from fear. "I am so lucky to have found someone who will love, cherish, and take care of me . . ."

The words felt like sandpaper grating in her mouth. She stumbled over them as she searched desperately for things to say. *Be nice. Have to fool him.*

Asher gripped her fingers tighter. When Allegra looked up at him, his eyes were roaming her body. She tried to swallow but couldn't seem to move. *If anyone traps you, you must fight.* Tigo and Finn's words were flashing across her brain. It was the only thing she could focus on. If rescue wasn't coming, then she was going to have to find a way to save both herself and Shirley.

"Um, your love is like the sun guiding the moon . . ." she stammered. She had no idea what she was saying at that point. She let her mouth spout nonsense as she took in every detail of Asher and the building they were in. The front door was locked, but she bet Asher had the key on him. Allegra also saw the bulge of a knife tucked into its sheath at his hip. "Love is like grass, constantly growing . . ." If she could just reach his knife.

"That's enough dear. Your love is overwhelming," Asher interrupted. "But I can't wait any longer to say the words I have dreamed about since I first saw you. I now pronounce us husband and wife. I may kiss the bride."

Allegra steeled herself against the reflex to back away as Asher pulled her forward and into his arms. His lips pressed against hers in a painful crushing as his tongue pressed into her mouth. Her throat tightened as it involuntarily gagged. Her body was rebelling against Asher even as her mind fought to control the fear.

His hands ran down her back and clasped her bottom. Allegra couldn't stop the squeal, but luckily Asher was so lost in his own world he thought it was in pleasure. She placed her hands on his chest and moved them down as seductively as she could. His grip tightened as he forced her closer. Allegra struggled to stay calm. Fear was clouding her judgment and screaming for her to run. Instead of giving in, she ran her hands lower. She felt it then, the top of the knife.

Suddenly Asher was jerked from her body. Her fingers grasped at his shirt instead of the knife. Asher looked down, and in that split second he figured out what Allegra was trying to do. A large coral purse swung again and connected with Asher's shoulder. Shirley stood on wobbly chicken legs swinging her massive purse. Her face was white as she swung again and again as if her purse were a lasso.

"Don't. Touch. My. Girl." Shirley shouted with all the force she could as she swung the purse above her head.

Asher took a step back and ignored the crazy old bat. Instead he looked into Allegra's eyes. Her hand was still outstretched. That bitch had lied to him. She was trying to take his control away. She was trying to escape him. No. He couldn't allow such an affront. Not from some poor trash that lucked into fortune and then played with men's emotions. She would pay.

He looked at Allegra with such hatred, fear overtook her, and she stepped away from him. Yes, he wanted her to feel his power. "What were you reaching for, Allegra?" he asked in a voice that caused her eyes to go wide.

"Y-y-you . . ." Allegra stammered. She tried to flash him a seductive smile but it was more of a grimace. *That lying bitch.* Anger washed over him. His heart hardened. She was just like the others. Well, he showed them and he'd show her.

"Oh, you want me, do you? Can't wait to fulfill your wifely duties? Fine." Asher shrugged out of his jacket and ripped his bow tie from his neck. He'd take her right here and now. Her screams would bring him even more enjoyment than the others had.

Allegra shot a quick glance at the knife. Everything had changed, and now she knew she was in a fight for her life. Madness had overtaken Asher as he took off his jacket and started unbuttoning his shirt. The knife was right where

Allegra had seen it, and she'd almost had it in her grip.

He followed her gaze and smiled, his teeth bared to her. "Oh, is that what you want?" He pulled the knife from its sheath, and Allegra took another step back.

The sharp steel blade glinted in the candlelight as he held it in his hand showing off. *Thwack!* Shirley's purse connected with his head again. He staggered back, and Allegra lunged.

She grabbed the hand holding the knife. Her thumb dug into the soft flesh between Asher's thumb and pointer finger. Her fingers curled in a death grip across his knuckles. She stepped to the side to avoid being cut as she pulled across his hand, causing his arm to twist. At the same time, she leapt behind him and slammed her left hand into his hyperextended elbow. It was a move Tigo had made her practice over and over again.

The knife fell the floor, and Asher screamed out in pain. Her victory was short-lived. Asher twisted toward her and swung. His desperate punch hit its mark as her head snapped to the side. She dropped her hold and staggered sideways. The long satin dress twisted in her legs, and she went down hard.

Asher shook out his arm and slowly bent down to pick up the knife. He was so focused on her that he didn't see Shirley sneaking up behind him. She took a step forward and swung her purse with enough force to send her spinning. The purse slammed him in the back of the head, and Asher went down on one knee.

Allegra lunged awkwardly forward and grabbed at his head. Her only thought was to dig her thumb into his eye. He'd never look at another woman like he had her. Her fingers turned into claws as she raked her nails down his face, blood bubbling to the surface.

He backhanded her across the cheek before she had a chance to counter with another attack. With a war cry, Shirley leapt onto him. She wrapped her arms around his neck and held on as he fought with her. Asher staggered to stand, and Allegra reached down and ripped the bottom of her gown as best she could. She got to her feet again and landed a solid kick to his groin. Asher went down on his knees hard, but he took Shirley with him.

Allegra zeroed in on the knife sitting forgotten on the white satin floor. It was to the left of where Asher was holding his balls and sucking in air while Shirley pummeled his head. She ran and dove—just like a player sliding into second base—on the slick material. The material gave way, and the candelabra behind her fell backward with a crash. Allegra reached her hand out. She almost had it. But a sharp pain stopped her as her head was wrenched backward. Asher's hand tangled into her hair as he tried to rip it from her head. As he pulled her head back, she saw Shirley lying where he must have tossed her off his back.

Automatically, her hands went to cover his as she tried to stop the pain. He flung her backward like a ragdoll and picked up the knife. Allegra and Shirley scrambled to their feet as they stared at Asher. Pure evil filled his eyes; he stared them down.

"I loved you, but you never loved me, did you?"

Allegra was so over being nice. She felt the anger start at her toes and rise through her body until she was trembling with adrenaline. "No. You're a self-important brat who only cares about himself. I could never love someone like you," she spat.

"You're just like the others. I thought you were so special, but you're just like the other whores. Your panties get wet for the likes of Harry and Finn. Well, Harry's dead because of you. I slit his throat from ear to ear, just like I'm going to do to you and then Finn. You're just a *whore*! Just like the rest of them."

"NO!" Allegra yelled back as she stepped forward, his eyes round in surprise as she advanced toward him. "You don't get to hurt anyone else ever again."

He moved so fast she didn't even process what he was doing. He reached out, grabbed Shirley, and sank the knife into her hip. Allegra felt her heart stop as she watched Shirley crumple to the floor in slow motion. When she looked up, Asher stood over the old woman with a demented smile on his face, holding the bloodied knife in his hand.

"See, I'll hurt whoever I want."

All Allegra saw was red. She leapt at Asher. She didn't feel the knife slicing into her arm. All she saw was Shirley not moving on the floor as Allegra balled her hands into fists and let them fly.

Mallory was out of the car and opening the trunk before it seemed to have stopped. She tossed a gun at Finn before sliding a second gun into her back and a knife into her boot. She grabbed her Glock 42 and flipped on the red laser sight. Terrell appeared out of the shadows.

"Gun?" she asked without looking up.

"Got one."

"Is it legal?"

"Um, maybe I need one then."

"Take whatever you want," Mallory motioned to the open silver gun case. "I'm taking the front. Finn, take the side door. Terrell, take the back door. Wait exactly two minutes and then bust the doors down. I got lead," Mallory said before leaving them staring after her.

Finn gripped the gun in his hand as he and Terrell ran past Mallory, who was walking with deadly precision for the front door. His mother had spent her whole life keeping guns out of his hands and, as his hand tightened around it, he knew for Allegra he would use it. For Allegra, he would rip Asher apart.

"NO!"

Finn stopped in his tracks. That was Allegra. His body was slammed with fear as he sprinted to the side door. He didn't care if he was early. As soon as he reached the door, he put his foot on it and broke it down.

Allegra felt Asher's nose crunch beneath her hand. It didn't stop her, though. She punched, jabbed, kicked, and scratched—anything to hurt him.

"Dirty WHORE!" Asher screamed as his hand came up to his bloody nose. "Enough!" His punch connected with her face, and Allegra saw stars. She fell hard. Before she could even catch her breath, Asher was on top of her with the knife in hand.

She struggled, but he had her arms pinned at her sides, her back on the floor, and his knees on either side of her as he sat across her hips. He looked down at her and smiled. Blood dripped from his face and in between his teeth, giving him a look of walking death.

"That wasn't very nice, Allegra. And I chose you for your sweet compliance. I see now I was wrong. But, if I don't get you, then no one will." Asher leaned down until his face was right in front of hers, the knife pressing loosely against her throat.

Allegra struggled. She kicked, but her legs couldn't connect with anything. She tried to free her arms, but they were pinned. That left one weapon, her head. She just had to get him a little closer.

"Too bad you'll never have me either. You'll never know how lucky Finn was to have something you'll never have." Allegra smiled innocently at him. "Aw, poor Asher, never to know my love. Finn has it, though. He has my heart and my soul," Allegra dropped her voice, and Asher leaned the rest of the way forward to hear her, "and my body."

Allegra snapped her head forward with all the strength she could muster. She felt her eyes roll back as her head connected with his. Her vision swam as she watched him bend back with the force of her hit.

The knife nicked her neck as he brought both hands to his face. Allegra fought with all she had and managed to wiggle one arm free. She went straight for the knife. She heard crashing and smelled smoke, but it didn't register. All her attention was focused on the fight between Asher and her for the knife in his hand.

She felt her arm shaking with exhaustion as she gripped his wrist. She was going to lose. Asher had both hands on the hilt of the knife and was pushing it straight down toward her throat. In that instant she knew she wasn't going to come out of this alive. Images of her mother, her sisters, and her friends flashed through her mind. But it was the memory of Finn holding her tight to him—his hand running through her hair as he whispered his love for her—that would be her last image.

Finn kicked the door in and rushed into the darkness of the building. He smelled smoke and followed the sounds of music through an empty storage room. He pushed through another door and entered what looked to be a break room.

Voices. He heard Allegra shouting and screaming. He

knocked over chairs as he raced forward. He slammed a swinging door open and skidded to a stop. Fire was licking the side of the building. An altar was set up in the middle of the room where a bloody Asher was on top of an equally bloody Allegra with a knife to her throat. The world stopped spinning. Finn aimed his gun, put his finger on the trigger, but then a blast echoed through the building.

Allegra felt the tip of the blade cutting into the soft skin of her throat. She was going to die. She knew it. At least Finn knew she loved him. She would always love him. The image of Finn pressing gentle kisses on her face shifted. *Fight,* his image said to her. Allegra blinked. If these were going to be her last moments, she wasn't going to go out nicely. She was going to fight, just as Finn had taught her.

She screamed at Asher, she didn't even know what, just screamed. She fought with everything she had. Suddenly Asher swayed, and with a look of complete disbelief, fell onto her. *Fight*! She grabbed his shirt and shoved. She blindly fought to reach between their bodies and grab his knife.

She heard her name then. It was coming from somewhere in the building. Asher lay cheek to cheek with her, and she turned her head away from him to find the source of the call.

"Finn!" He was running toward her, gun in hand. She fought to shove Asher off her. She had to get to Finn.

She lifted her head over Asher's shoulder and saw Mallory walking toward her. Her face was tense, her blue eyes narrowed and unmoving. The gun in her hand was still trained on Asher. A red laser from the gun highlighted the hole Mallory had put in the back of Asher's head.

It was over. Allegra let her head collapse back onto the

ground. “Shirley! Someone check on Shirley!” she screamed as the memory that caused her vision to turn red came back to her.

“I’m still here,” Shirley’s shaky voice called out.

“Oh, thank God! I think I’m going to pass out now,” Allegra managed to say before all the strength left her body, and the world turned black.

Chapter Twenty-Two

Finn closed the distance between him and Allegra in a blink of an eye. He reached down and grabbed Asher's shoulders and pulled him off her. There was blood everywhere. Finn frantically tossed Asher's dead body aside and pressed his fingers to Allegra's throat. He felt a pulse.

"She's alive!" he called out, but he didn't need to. Mallory and Terrell were already there.

Mallory was kneeling next to Asher and shook her head. "He's not."

"And just who are you? My, you're a strong one," Shirley managed weakly as Terrell helped prop her up and pressed his hand against the gash in her hip.

Sirens wailed in the distance. Finn ran his hands over Allegra's body. Her face was swelling, there were a couple of small cuts on her throat, and a large one on her arm. He picked up a piece of satin wedding dress from the floor and tied it around her arm.

"Come back to me, sweetheart. I love you. You're safe."

"But, you all aren't," Mallory said with all seriousness. "Hand me the guns. I don't want you all getting into any kind of trouble."

"And what a sexy gun you have," Shirley murmured, her eyes starting to droop.

Finn couldn't help the laughter. Right there in the middle of the blood-soaked dais with fire spreading, he laughed. Terrell looked utterly shocked at the eighty-plus-year-old white-haired woman with a death grip on a bright orange purse.

"FBI!" Agent Hectoria yelled as she rushed in with backup. She lowered her weapon and took in the scene. "Get some firemen in here!"

Allegra felt hot. Was she in hell? Dear Lord, her mother had warned her to get to church, but she hadn't. Was this her punishment? Her mother also told her to wear clean underpants in case of an accident. Maybe hell was a better place for her. She'd stopped being nice and gotten killed with day-old panties. Hell would protect her from her mother's lecture.

"Allegra, sweetheart, come back to me."

Oh, Finn. Hell was a horrible place. It was hot, she had on dirty underwear, and she was tortured with images of Asher straddling her with a knife at her throat. Then Satan taunted her by tossing in Finn's voice calling to her.

"Allegra! Open your eyes. You're safe, sweetheart. I've got you."

Allegra struggled to open her eyes. When she did, images of flames filled her vision. She promptly slammed them shut again. "You're not nice, Satan!"

"Satan? Allegra, it's me, Finn. Asher is dead, and the warehouse is on fire. I'm going to lift you, but I need to know if you're hurt anywhere else."

Allegra cracked open an eye. "I'm not in hell?"

Finn came into view and smiled down at her. "You're an angel. We'll be old and in heaven together, but not for a really, really long time. For the time being, let's get you out of here. Are you hurt anywhere else?"

"My arm hurts, my face hurts . . . well, everything hurts, but I'm alive," Allegra said with her patented optimism. She tried to see out of an eye that was swelling closed. "Is that Asher?"

Allegra felt her hands tighten into fists as her body prepared to fight. But then two men put him on a stretcher. Mallory stood behind him and watched as Agent Hectoria organized the evacuation of the building. Two men with cameras took pictures, one man took video, and firefighters were spraying the fire with water and foam. She looked to the other side and saw two EMTs lifting Shirley onto a stretcher.

Mallory stepped forward. "How're you doing, Allegra?"

"Never better. Did you kill him?" Mallory gave a single nod of her head. "Thank you. But, Mallory," Allegra called as Mallory turned to leave, "and Agent Hectoria."

Finn slid his arms under her back and knees. He lifted her to him, and she clung to him. "We need to get out of here, sweetheart."

"No," Allegra yelled again. For someone who had hardly ever said that word, she was getting used to it. "This is important. Mallory, Agent, there's something else Asher said."

She felt Finn stop and turn toward Mallory and Agent Hectoria. They hurried toward her as the video man stepped closer to film her.

"What did he say?" the agent asked.

"He said there were *others*. He referred to the *rest of them*."

Finn swore. Mallory looked like she wanted to shoot Asher again. Agent Hectoria gave her a quick look before reaching for her phone. "Everyone, clear the building," she yelled before dialing.

"Come on, Allegra, let's get you to the hospital and call your family."

Allegra turned herself over to Finn and the EMTs. Everything was blurry. Her eye was swelling shut, her head rang, and exhaustion was overtaking her quickly. She remembered answering questions for an FBI agent and being wheeled into X-ray. Finally, she was settled in a hospital bed. Her eyes closed almost instantly, and she let sleep take over.

Mallory stood in the hall of the hospital outside Allegra's room and handed her gun to Agent Hectoria. With all the chaos, the agent hadn't asked for it until then. They would test it for ballistics to confirm it was the gun used in the shooting. For as long as she lived, Mallory would never forget the cold fury that overtook her as she leveled the gun and pulled the trigger without a second's hesitation.

"You saved a lot of lives today. But, I expect you'll see a lot of blowback from the Woodcrofts," Agent Hectoria said as she put the gun into an evidence bag.

"I would do anything for those women in there." Mallory gestured to where Shirley and Allegra were, next to each other in the hospital emergency room.

"It's not just them. We're getting reports from LA, New York, and Miami of murdered women that fit Asher's MO." Agent Hectoria let out a sigh. "We also uncovered at least eight rape cases that suddenly disappeared. It looks like he was spending money on more than wild parties. He was paying off his victims or making them disappear. We're hoping some of them went off the grid on their own and will come forward as news of his death breaks."

"I had no idea. I've known him for years." Mallory shook her head. What had she missed? She felt she could have prevented some of this.

"Don't beat yourself up about it. As you know, money can conceal a lot about a person's past. Can't it?"

"It can provide an excellent cover," Mallory agreed.

"Well, the FBI will stand behind you if the Woodcrofts do any more than blast you publicly. We'll release our own statement after we talk to some of the families in the other cities. In that statement, we'll tell the other victims they are safe to come out of hiding. I just hope there are some who escaped. At last count, there were six women whose murder investigations are now being reopened."

"Please keep me updated. Let me know if there is anything I can do for the victims or their families."

Mallory didn't watch the agent walk away. She stared at the curtains and waited for him to come. She had sensed him the moment he walked into the hospital. The twin doors to the lobby opened, and he walked in. His hands were in his jeans pockets and the V-neck sweater clung to his wide shoulders. Mallory rolled her eyes and quickly clenched her fingers into tight fists before relaxing her whole body. Her heart had broken, and it would never be repaired. She believed there was nothing left to hurt if she didn't have a heart. For years, she'd turned that part of her off and vowed to never feel again.

"I guess I owe you a thank-you," he said, stopping next to her.

She could feel the heat coming off his body and fought the urge to move closer. "I'd do anything for her," she said, never taking her eyes from the fabric drape surrounding

Allegra's bed.

"Thank you for saving Allegra."

"You're welcome, Reid."

Reid pursed his lips and disappeared behind the curtain. The rest of the Simpson family would be here soon, and she didn't want to be. Her sister was safe. Mallory smiled at the blue drape and walked down the long hallway by herself.

"You are the sexiest man I've ever seen. Come on, just give me a little peek. For a sick old woman."

"You want a pity strip?" A deep voice floated into her room.

"You betcha."

The deep voice chuckled from behind the fabric room divider. "I need to check on Miss Simpson. Behave yourself while I'm gone."

Allegra opened her eyes and saw Finn sitting on the corner of her bed and Reid standing against the wall with his arms crossed over his chest. They were both staring at the blue drape as it was drawn back. The escort they met at Elle's bachelorette party walked in.

She felt her face flush as she looked quickly between Aiden and the men in the room. Reid and Finn wore a look of utter confusion.

"How are you doing, Miss Simpson?"

His voice almost caused her to shudder. Damn, he was hot. "G-g-good," she stuttered and then giggled. "It's hot. I mean, nice to see you again, Aiden. Did Shirley call you?" Finn shot her a dark look and took her hand in his. She felt the blush deepen on her cheeks. Those scrubs had to be painted on.

"No, I'm your doctor." Allegra giggled again. "No, really. I'm your doctor . . . Dr. Aiden Starr."

The blue panel was pushed aside, and Allegra felt her mouth drop open. Oh, she was going to get Shirley for this. An equally hot doctor walked in looking at a chart.

"Miss Simpson, I'm Dr. Barry Stein. I'm here to consult on your lacerations." She giggled again, and Dr. Stein looked up and froze.

"Is that Barry?" Shirley called as Dr. Stein blanched.

"It's not what it looks like . . ." he said quickly.

"Someone better tell me what this is, because by the way Allegra is giggling and what I overheard between Dr. Starr there and Shirley, I'm not liking what I'm thinking." Finn stood up as Barry and Aiden shot nervous glances at each other.

"Don't worry, Finn. Shirley hired them to cheer me up. We met them at Elle's bachelorette party."

Finn looked up to the heavens as if asking for patience. "I'm not surprised Shirley would order escorts. But at the hospital?"

Shirley and Allegra giggled again and Aiden cleared his throat. "Actually, we are doctors. Our weekend activities help us pay off our massive student loans."

"That's not the only thing that's massive," Shirley shot out from behind her curtain.

Allegra snorted. "Here I was worried about you, Shirley."

"Nah, I got me one of those nice titanium hips three years ago. The knife bounced right off it. And having Dr. Sexyscrubs here is worth the couple of stitches I needed."

Finn groaned, and Reid hid his laughter behind a cough.

"Maybe they should turn down her morphine drip," Reid whispered.

Allegra just giggled again. "I don't think it would help."

"Thank you, Shirley," Aiden called out. "Now, Allegra, Dr. Stein is going to stitch you up so that you won't have any scars. He's really good at what he does."

"He sure is! Ask him to take his shirt off while he's sewing," Shirley called out.

"Really, Shirley?" Finn responded.

"Crapola, I didn't know Finn was there. You could have warned a girl," Shirley said, sounding only slightly embarrassed.

The curtain opened as Margaret, Elle, Drake, Bree, and Logan hurried into the room. Margaret stopped first at seeing Aiden and Barry. Allegra just watched the pile-up. Only Bree and Logan didn't seem surprised. Her mother sputtered, Elle suddenly had interest in her cell phone, and Drake just looked confused as to why the women had suddenly stopped.

"Mom," Allegra said, finally taking pity on her. "This is Dr. Aiden Starr and Dr. Barry Stein. We met them at Elle's bachelorette party. Well, they happen to be on call tonight and are taking good care of Shirley and me."

"Oh," Margaret's eyes flitted to where Shirley was. "Well, bless your hearts."

Finn sat with Allegra as Dr. Barry stitched her up. He held her hand the whole time, not wanting to let her go. When Dr. Barry was finished and Allegra's X-rays had come back clear, he helped her check out. Her family was waiting in the lobby along with Shirley who was happily being escorted in a wheelchair by a strapping transport assistant.

"Oh, honey!" Margaret hurried forward and wrapped her in another hug. Finn stepped back and let Margaret fuss. She was going to take Shirley home with her and take care of her after Finn promised to do the same with Allegra.

The doors to the hospital opened as Terrell and Willa ran inside. "Finn! Oh Lordy child!" His mother covered her mouth as she tried to hide her gasp when she saw Allegra.

"It looks worse than it feels, Willa. Well, at least I hope it does from everyone's expressions. I have to admit I haven't wanted to look in a mirror."

Finn couldn't blame her. One eye was swollen shut, and she had sets of stitches on her neck. There was still blood in her hair. Some of it hers, some of it Asher's. Her wrist was wrapped where he had grabbed her so hard he had cracked the bone. Her arm was bandaged from the stab wound, and bruises were appearing on her face, arms, and body. Every time he looked at her, he cursed Mallory for shooting Asher. He wanted to kill him with his bare hands.

His mother turned to Margaret and smiled reassuringly. "I'm Willa Williams, Finn's mother. I promise I raised him with better manners than to forget to introduce us."

Allegra squeezed his hand, and he felt her laughing quietly from her wheelchair.

"Oh, I'm so pleased to meet you. Your son is like my own. I'm sure we'll be fast friends," Margaret said as she smiled brightly.

"I feel the same way about your sweet daughter. God only blessed me with one child, but now I feel as if I have two. See, Finn's father passed when he was just an infant," his mother said sadly.

Finn knew it hurt her to talk about his father. He had been a firefighter and had died during a building collapse.

His mother had never loved another.

"I understand completely. My dear husband left us nine years ago." Margaret took Willa's hand in hers, and they bonded instantly.

"I must say, I was surprised when Terrell told me Finn was in the ER with Allegra. I didn't think they allowed anyone but family back there." Both he and Allegra groaned, but that didn't stop his mother from continuing. "It would be different if they were engaged . . ."

Margaret clucked her tongue and shook her head. "I know. I was surprised, too. Allegra knew the doctor so he let Finn in. I swear, young people these days don't know a good thing when he's holding onto her hand."

Both mothers turned and stared at Finn and Allegra's clasped hands.

"I couldn't agree more. Why waste time when you know you're meant to be together?" Willa asked.

Elle, Drake, Bree, Logan, and Reid stood next to Terrell, looking as if they were about to burst with laughter.

"I know I met *the* one," Terrell said with pleasure lacing his rough voice. "A blond angel with a streak of the devil in her."

Finn saw Reid stop laughing and straighten up.

"Is that so?" Willa asked, taking her attention away from Finn and Allegra. "Is it that nice woman who helped our dear Allegra?"

"Mallory Westin," Terrell said a little dreamily. "When I saw her slide that knife into her boot, I fell in love."

"Don't talk about her like that," Reid snapped.

Finn and everyone else looked surprised by his outburst. Only Elle looked curiously between Terrell and Reid as if she were figuring something out for the first time.

Margaret tilted her head, and Finn saw her eyes narrow

at her son. "And why not, dear? Mallory's single, after all. And she does handle a knife very well. You should have seen her carve the Thanksgiving turkey the other year—the year you were in Europe and couldn't make it home."

Reid froze for a minute, and Finn saw his mask fall back into place. Finn looked down at Allegra whose eyes had similarly narrowed at her brother. They were like sharks smelling blood in the water.

Reid rolled his eyes nonchalantly. "She's more than a knife. You can't forget she's a Westin," he said in a stuffy accent.

Terrell shrugged. "So? I'm not going to discriminate because she's rich."

"It's not you that you have to worry about. No matter how much Mallory likes to play on the wrong side of the tracks, deep down she's stuck in her debutante world."

"I'm not afraid of a challenge. And man, did you see how she handled her car? It makes you wonder how she'd handle her man."

Finn saw it coming, but Terrell didn't. Reid's fist connected with Terrell's jaw, and he went down hard. Finn, Drake, Logan, and Bree jumped into the fray, but it was Finn's mother who got to them first.

"Now, boys. Mallory is a person, not some toy to fight over." Willa held her hands between them as they stared each other down. "Now, Terrell, I've taught you better than that. Let's go home. I have some gutters that need to be cleaned. It will give you some time to think about what you said."

"Yes, ma'am."

Margaret put her hands on her hips and came to stand next to Willa in between the two towering men. "And Reid Simpson, you never hit a man like that just because he said something you don't like. Now, shake hands and go home. You can help me get Shirley upstairs."

"I'm always up for a handsome young man carrying me," Shirley chimed in to break the tension.

Terrell and Reid reluctantly shook hands and followed Margaret and Willa out the door. Allegra snickered first, and then the rest of them joined in.

"What was that about?" Bree asked as they walked out into the parking lot.

"I don't know," Allegra answered as they watched Margaret lecture Reid by his sports car.

"But it was interesting, that's for sure," Elle said with a look that told Finn she had an idea but wasn't ready to share. "Now, Leggy, how about you? Do you need anything?"

Allegra continued to watch Reid. She'd known something was going on; she just wondered what.

"Leggy?" Bree asked, and Allegra snapped back to her group.

"Sorry, what?"

Elle smiled gently. "Do you need anything?"

Allegra nodded. "Sleep. Lots and lots of sleep. I don't think I've really slept since this started. And food. I'm starving."

"We can help with that." Elle patted her shoulder and then took charge. "Finn, you take her to your home and put her to bed. Mallory and Agent Hectoria are sweeping your place again and then heading over to Asher's place to gather evidence to help find the other women he referred to. But, no worries, sis, you're safe now. Bree, you and Logan get some wine and maybe something stronger. Drake and I will get food and lots of it. I know all your favorites. Now, the important question . . . should I invite Aiden and Barry?"

Bree snorted. Drake and Logan didn't look happy as Allegra laughed. She laughed so hard tears started to come out of her one good eye. "Oh gosh, did you hear Shirley asking if he'd give her a pity strip?"

Soon the whole group was laughing, and Allegra felt the fear, depression, and anxiety lifting. It would be a long road to full recovery, but she was already well on her way.

Mallory stood next to Agent Hectoria and pointed to the vent. "There." She looked at Asher's computer screen and the images of Allegra and Finn. "And in the vent in the living room."

The FBI agents stood on ladders and pulled the small cameras from the vents. They had found the laptop in Asher's car. As soon as they broke the password, they had found the images from Allegra's old house, new house, and her condo in New York. The FBI office in New York City was currently taking those down as the Atlanta team worked.

"Okay, I think we got them all," an agent said as he put the cameras in evidence bags.

"There are just a few more things." Mallory went into Allegra's closet and found the gifts Asher had sent. They were all put into evidence bags and taken away.

"Thank you, Mallory. Do you need to talk to someone after the shooting?" Agent Hectoria asked.

"No. I'm okay."

Agent Hectoria looked at her, and Mallory could see the curiosity in her eyes. "You know, I pulled your file. Strange thing is, I didn't have clearance to look at it. In fact, the only person at the FBI with the clearance to see it is the director."

"Hmm, that is strange," Mallory murmured nonchalantly. Agent Hectoria just smiled and suddenly her sharp face softened. She was a lot younger than Mallory had originally thought. "When you have time, can you go meet with Agent Damien Wallace of the Secret Service? I think he'd like to hear your take on the case."

"Sure. The Woodcrofts are coming into the office. I need to meet with them first, and then I'll go see him."

Mallory watched her go and felt proud of her matchmaking efforts. Just because her heart was walled off didn't mean she didn't like to see others happily in love. Mallory turned and walked out the door. She needed a vacation—away from Atlanta and away from the man who had destroyed all hope of love for her.

Chapter Twenty-Three

Allegra looked into the mirror with relief. It had taken weeks, but the bruises were gone, the stitches were out, and the nightmares were fading. The Woodcrofts had decided against suing Mallory or the FBI. Deep down they had known something was not right with their son. With broken hearts, they escaped to Europe for the winter.

Seven more victims from all over the world had come forward with relief and told their stories of survival. There was a clear pattern. Asher would find a woman he was determined fate had placed in front of him. He would ask them out and sometimes they would say yes and sometimes not. If they said no, he stalked them and became obsessed with them.

Families of unsolved murders now had answers, and those victims who had survived now had closure. But it was not over; it never would be. It would get better, but Allegra would never forget the terror. Instead of succumbing to the fear, she spoke out about it. Her face, covered with bruises, graced the front of magazines all over the world showing that crime was universal. It didn't matter if a person was rich or poor, man or woman—it mattered that there were people out there willing to do everything possible to help them.

Allegra wrapped a scarf around her neck. She closed the door to the house when she heard the car engine approaching. The "For Sale" sign was set in the yard, and she felt comfortable leaving everything from the past behind. After all, her future had just arrived.

Finn opened the car door and stood up. He was in fitted jeans that hugged his athletic legs. The collar of his button-up shirt stuck out under a dark gray V-neck sweater as he turned to open her door.

"You ready for a romantic night out?" Finn asked before leaning down to kiss her lips.

"More than anything. Where are we going?"

"It's a surprise." Finn shot her a grin that made her melt into the seat.

They drove through Atlanta and out into the suburbs. "This is the way to Reid's newest hotel."

Finn just winked, but didn't answer her as he drove closer to Reid's hotel. It was almost done now. The grand opening was set for March. There was a soft opening in February over Valentine's Day weekend. Some of the most talked-about singers from Atlanta were scheduled to perform at both openings. Decorations were ordered and the chefs were planning mouth-watering meals to celebrate.

Finn turned into the entrance of the resort and drove down the tree-lined road toward the massive hotel that sat back behind the woods.

"Wow, the building looks amazing. This is the first time I've seen it without construction equipment everywhere." Allegra looked up at the antebellum resort stretching out among the green rolling hills and woods.

Finn drove past the resort and down toward the barns housing the horses guests could use to go trail riding or play polo. The sun was a warm orange as it began to sink behind the lake.

"Are we going riding?" Allegra asked when Finn parked.

"Nope," Finn grinned. He was clearly enjoying himself.

"Are you ever going to tell me?" she asked as he helped her from the car and walked to the trunk.

"Nope." Finn leaned down and pressed his lips softly to hers to quiet her questions. He reached in the truck and pulled out a thick blanket and a large wooden picnic basket.

"Oh!" Allegra looked to the lake and laced her arm with Finn's. "A sunset picnic. This is perfect."

"You got it. I figured after such a crazy couple of weeks some peace, quiet, and alone time would be just the thing for us. It's been too long since I had you all to myself."

Allegra rested her head on his shoulder as they made their way to the white gazebo, lit by tiny white lights, sitting on the edge of the lake. Finn spread the blanket on the wooden floor and set down the basket. The gazebo was lined with two curved benches in between the two entrances, one on the lawn side and the other on the lake side. Lifting up one of the lids on the bench, he pulled out two large pillows and handed them to Allegra. Then with a twist of a knob, two small fire pits roared to life on each side of the gazebo.

"This is so nice. Who knew Reid would think of something like this?"

"I know. I'm starting to think there's a lot to Reid we don't know. But, enough about your brother." Finn opened the picnic basket and brought out two mugs and a thermos. He opened it, and the smell of hot chocolate filled the air.

"Perfect for this crisp fall evening," Allegra said as she held out her mug. Finn poured and then took a seat on the blanket next to her.

Allegra sighed with contentment as she leaned back against his chest. Finn rested his head against hers, and they watched the sun begin to sink into the water. Ducks floated by, crickets chirped, and Allegra felt complete happiness and peace at last. She'd learned a lot about herself over the past year, but one thing was unwavering—how much she loved Finn. She knew now it was okay for her to stand up for herself if being nice didn't work. In fact, having confidence in herself was garnering her more respect, and certainly Finn enjoyed it when they were in bed together.

"It's only perfect because you are here with me," Finn said before tenderly placing a kiss on her temple.

"The only thing that would make this better is a slice of my mother's pie," Allegra teased.

Finn held up a finger to tell her to hold on and reached into the basket. He pulled out two pieces of pie and forks. "Your wish is my command."

"You are amazing!" Allegra grabbed the pie and groaned as the apple and cinnamon met her tongue. "What else do you have in there?"

"You'll just have to wait to find out." Finn pulled her against him as they watched the sunset.

Soon the sun disappeared from view, and the last rays of light winked out. The lights from the gazebo bathed them in a soft glow. Finn set his mug down and ran his fingers down Allegra's cheek. His heart beat strong and sure as he reached a hand into the picnic basket once more.

"With the sunset comes the end of a day, one that could have been bad, good, exhausting, or exhilarating. With sunset comes the feeling of home, being with the person you love, like we are doing tonight. A person who can share your day with you, a person to kiss away the bad days and celebrate the good. You're my sunset, my home, my love."

Finn pulled his hand from the picnic basket and held a pink diamond ring in his fingers. He heard Allegra gasp and saw the mug fall from her hands as he moved around to kneel in front of her. He held the ring forward and saw the tears streaming down her cheeks and over her smiling lips.

"It looks shiny and beautiful on the outside. Delicate, happy, *nice*." He grinned. "But on the inside, a diamond is one of the toughest objects found in nature—just like you. You're beautiful on the outside, but inside you're an amazing combination of strength and love. And somehow I was lucky enough to earn your love. Allegra Simpson, will you marry me?"

Allegra threw her arms around his neck and hugged him with all her strength. "Yes!" she called out as she buried her face in his neck. She pulled back, and he saw his happiness reflected in her eyes.

He cupped her face in his hands and tilted her lips to his. "I love you."

"I love you, too." The world disappeared as their lips met. They were home in each other's arms.

Epilogue

Allegra closed her eyes and threw the bouquet as hard as she could. The pink flowers tied with white satin ribbons disappeared over her head. She turned and saw the bouquet sailing through the air. Hands were reaching up for it, but it flew over them. It was a GBM, guided bouquet missile, and was aimed for the one person not reaching for it.

Allegra cringed as the bouquet suddenly plummeted from the sky and hit Mallory on the head before rolling off and into her arms. The group of excited singles on the dance floor groaned their disappointment while Mallory looked like she'd just stepped in a cow patty. Her nose wrinkled and her lip went up in a snarl as she looked down at the bouquet in her hands.

Finn came to stand next to Allegra and laughed. "Mallory looks thrilled."

"I've never seen that look on her face before. She's had her society smile plastered on all day. I guess she just doesn't like weddings." Allegra shrugged and then turned to her husband. "You aren't going to do anything embarrassing when you remove my garter, are you?"

"Who, me? Why would you think that?" he asked a little too innocently.

"Oh, I don't know. Maybe because Terrell and Shirley

pulled you over a minute ago, and Shirley bared her teeth and shook her head as if attacking something with her teeth."

Finn and Allegra both looked at Shirley, standing next to Terrell. Her walker was decorated in white tulle and a banner reading *I'll be your Wedding Hook-up*.

"Okay, so maybe she suggested I detour from the traditional garter removal."

"Hmmph. Be good down there," Allegra hissed as she took her seat in a chair on the dance floor.

"Sweetheart, I'm always good down here." He smirked before running his hand up her leg.

Allegra's faced flushed as his fingers skimmed their way up to her garter. His finger hooked under it and rubbed back and forth before sliding it down.

"When can we leave?" Allegra asked in a whisper.

"As soon as I throw this blasted thing." Finn stood up and tossed the garter.

"Nice throw, Williams. Still think you're in baseball?" Allegra teased as the garter went flying.

Finn turned around, and Allegra slipped her hand into his. Jasper Hale, the new owner of the Golden Eagles, neatly sidestepped the garter sailing through the air. Jasper had turned out to be a lot like Drake. He was quiet, rich, and not out for attention. He'd become friends with the family after renegotiating Kane's contract with Finn. Meanwhile, Terrell made a flying leap for the garter. It hit his finger and slingshot to the man downing a shot of amber liquor. Allegra squeezed Finn's hand as she watched the garter nail her brother in his face.

"Oh, this should be very interesting," Allegra murmured as the wedding coordinator pulled Mallory and Reid from the crowd for their obligatory dance.

"Maybe we should stay for just a few more minutes," Finn said as they hurried from the dance floor. "But that doesn't mean I can't hook up with you in the shadows."

"I'm definitely good with that. Look at how well we're doing. We are going to rock at this marriage business," Allegra joked as they slid into the shadows, her hands already reaching for him as the music started up.

Mallory refused to move. "Come on. The woman who catches the bouquet has to dance with the man who catches the garter," the perky coordinator said as she tugged at Mallory's arm.

"If she's too afraid to dance with me . . ." Reid shrugged and tossed back another drink.

"Too afraid?" Mallory shook off the coordinator and grabbed Reid's hand in hers as Marvin Gaye's "Let's Get It On" started playing. It had to be this song. Could it get any worse? But she would never back down from a challenge and certainly not one issued by Reid Simpson.

Mallory felt his hand cup hers and his other wrap around her waist. "No, you were never afraid of anything. Or at least that's what I thought. But then again, it goes to show—you can't win every hand."

"Not now, Reid. We're at Allegra's wedding. You didn't want to hear what I had to say before. Do you really want to hear it now?"

"Nope. I've learned not to believe a single word from your luscious lips."

Mallory forced herself to swallow as she looked out into the crowd watching them. She smiled serenely and let him lead her around the floor. Let's get it on, indeed, she thought. Heck, there were lots of attractive men here tonight. It just wouldn't be Reid who she went home with.

"You look tan," Reid said so quietly she almost missed it.

"I've been in the Caribbean for the past month. I was meeting with contacts and such." This was the most normal conversation they'd had in fifteen years.

"I'm visiting my European holdings before the hotel here opens in March."

"I know. Your mother told me," Mallory said as the song neared the end.

"I don't want you there. This is the last time I'll have to see you. No more weddings, no more family moments where you intrude. This is it, Mallory. It would be great if you took another extended business trip. Atlanta isn't big enough for both of us, and this is *my* family, not yours."

Mallory felt a pain in her chest. He couldn't take away her family. But what he said was true. The Simpsons weren't her real family, even if they were more of a family to her than her own. The pain in her chest pulsed. She reached into the top of her bra and pulled out her phone as the music ended.

I have something you'll want. The plane is waiting for you.

Mallory looked up from the text from Ahmed, the former head of security for the Prince of Rahmi, a small island country in the Middle East. They had a history together that looked as if it were about to repeat itself. "Well, it looks like you got your wish." Mallory stepped out of Reid's arms and walked off the dance floor. She didn't look back as she left her life behind her once more.

Other Books by Kathleen Brooks

***Thanks for reading. Be sure to get the next great book from Kathleen Brooks as soon as it goes live by signing up on her notification list below:*

www.kathleen-brooks.com/new-release-notifications/

If you are new to the writings of Kathleen Brooks, then you will definitely want to try her Bluegrass Series books set in the wonderful fictitious town of Keeneston, KY. Here is a list of all of Kathleen's books in order:

<u>Bluegrass Series</u>

Bluegrass State of Mind

Risky Shot

Dead Heat

<u>Bluegrass Brothers Series</u>

Bluegrass Undercover

Rising Storm

Secret Santa, A Bluegrass Novella

Acquiring Trouble

Relentless Pursuit

Secrets Collide

Final Vow

<u>Bluegrass Singles</u>

All Hung Up

Bluegrass Dawn

Rose Sister novella collection due out mid-to-late 2015

<u>Women of Power Series</u>

Chosen for Power

Built for Power

Fashioned for Power

Destined for Power – coming April 6th, 2015

About the Author

Kathleen Brooks is a New York Times, Wall Street Journal, and USA Today bestselling author. Kathleen's stories are romantic suspense featuring strong female heroines, humor, and happily-ever-afters. Her Bluegrass Series and follow-up Bluegrass Brothers Series feature small town charm with quirky characters that have captured the hearts of readers around the world.

Kathleen is an animal lover who supports rescue organizations and other non-profit organizations such as Friends and Vets Helping Pets whose goals are to protect and save our four-legged family members.

Email Notice of New Releases:
www.kathleen-brooks.com/new-release-notifications/

Kathleen's Website:
www.kathleen-brooks.com

Facebook Page:
www.facebook.com/KathleenBrooksAuthor

Twitter:
www.twitter.com/BluegrassBrooks

Goodreads:
www.goodreads.com/author/show/5101707.Kathleen_Brooks

Made in the USA
San Bernardino, CA
25 November 2017